BREAKING THE SHADOW'S GRIP

Martha Wolowicz

First Printing......................................April, 2008

Breaking the Shadow's Grip © 2008
Martha Wolowicz
All rights reserved

ISBN # 978-0-615-20485-7

Because this is a book of fiction, any name or character resembling persons living or dead is purely coincidental. All incidents, locations or scientific assumptions are products of the author's imagination and are used fictionally.

Published in the U.S.A. by:
Inspired Word Publications
Martha Wolowicz

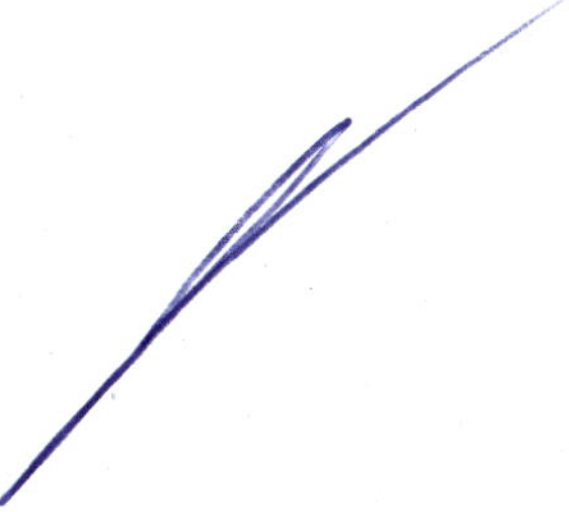

PROLOGUE

Sarah, despite her eighty-five years, managed to stand on a small stool to get a better look at the weathered box on her closet shelf. She sighed deeply. Soon, most assuredly *quite* soon, she would have to tell Abigail the gruesome story and give her the document that had been hidden in that box for twenty years. How Abigail would react to the unthinkable news was a constant apprehension for Sarah…but, it was now time.

Chapter One

The young woman forced herself to leave her car and trudge up the slippery walkway leading to the graves. She hated to come here. Even after a year, the intense heartache was still there. On each occasion her cemetery pilgrimage gave rise to the sorrow that enveloped the precious memories of her loving parents.

Once again the question plagued her. *Why were Mom and Dad so determined to talk to me that night? My birthday, even my twenty-first birthday, wasn't that important that they had to travel those treacherous roads in the rain. They said they had something to tell me about the past and my adoption...which was strange as they always avoided the subject before. Why was that night so critical? I'll never understand it, never. And, now it's too late.*

Abigail's thoughts released the flood of tears she had been trying to stifle as she continued walking, until up ahead she could see the graves with their simple black headstone, shiny from the falling mist. Though the graves were still yards in front of her up a small knoll, she was able to discern the professional cut of the names in the stone, and those names cut deep into her heart.

"Peter and Dorcas Demitt, Loving Parents and Grandparents. At Rest with God."

They are at rest, but I'm still struggling to find peace, she wept as she neared the graves. *I miss them so much.*

Abigail Demitt knelt on the wet grass and lovingly stroked the black etched stone. She envisioned her mother as she ironed the drapes Abigail had picked out for her very first house. Her mother had always been there when she needed her. It was as if she knew what Abigail needed before she was even asked. They had a unique relationship, more like best friends, often lunching together and jabbering like two school girls. Happy times...painful memories.

Dad was one-of-a-kind too, she recalled. *He had such gentleness and strength and I always knew he would be there for me no matter what happened in my life. He and mom gave me such love. They were always so concerned about me...hovering over me to make sure I was all right.* On this day of bittersweet memories, Abby, as she was often called, thought about the unusual concern her parents had each time she even had a sniffle. But, that was only a remembrance now.

She had no idea how long she had been kneeling at the gravesite when she felt a gentle touch on her shoulder. She looked up from her nostalgia into the concerned eyes of her brother Josh.

Josh was six years older than Abby's twenty-two years and was already established as a preacher at the small Community Christian Church in Vesta. He was a natural athlete often gaining acclaim for his abilities even though it wasn't a struggle for him. He kept himself fit and trim which emphasized his good looks. His sense of humor and sincere compassion for others endeared him to everyone he met, and Abby found his genuine sense of peace to have an immediate calming effect on her.

"Oh Josh, I'm so glad you're here," she said smiling for the first time that afternoon. She held out her arm for his help to stand and did her best to wipe the wet soil off her knees. It was then she saw that Josh wasn't alone. A little behind and to the left of her brother was his friend, David. Abby was somewhat embarrassed by her tear-stained face and muddy knees, but at the same time quite pleased to see him.

She and David had known each other since David moved to Vesta to attend high school. He and Josh became fast friends and shared interests in various team sports. Abby admired him through the starry-eyes of a grade school girl and coyly vied for his attention whenever he came to their house to see Josh. She secretly dreamed of being his girl friend and often played Abby and David with her Barbie and Ken.

Abby lost track of him when he left to attend college and then law school. His parents left shortly after David and became missionaries in South America. Abby finished high school in a whirl of activities and friends and began her own college education for her BS degree in nursing. When David returned to Vesta as a young lawyer, Abby had just begun her job as a nurse at Vesta Memorial Hospital. Whenever any of the nurses talked about David McNeal, it was generally accepted that he was a "hunk." His thick sandy hair carefully framed a classically handsome face, and he had a smile that made the girls tingle.

David had been asked to join a small law firm in Vesta, and it was then he and Josh renewed their friendship…and little Abigail, who was no longer little but an alarmingly beautiful young woman with cascading red hair and emerald green highlights in her deep blue eyes, began to notice him again. By all appearances David was interested in her as well, but before they were able to pursue that mutual interest, the horrendous car accident took the lives of Abby's parents and any future plans were put on an indefinite hold.

But today because David was here, Abby's visit to the cemetery was taking on a more positive outlook and after hugging her brother warmly, she turned and greeted David with a smile she hoped wasn't too expressive of her delight at seeing him.

"Hi, Abby. Thought I'd tag along with Josh when he decided to come out and check to see if you were here. Hope you don't mind?"

"Oh no, I'm glad to see you."

David became somewhat flustered now that he was face to face with Abby once again, and stammered a moment. "W-w-we were, ah, working on a project and when Josh said he was going to look for you here, I just figured it was a good time to talk to you. Maybe catch you for a minute when we get back to the parking lot?"

Abby was more than interested, and without hesitation agreed immediately. The sun was beginning to sneak out of its hiding place as Abby glanced at her brother's smiling face.

The three of them left the gravesite a short time later dodging the frequent mud puddles. Abby turned and glanced up the knoll once again at the gleaming stone that symbolized the past. Josh and David quickly grabbed her arms and carefully steered her down the slippery path. Her sudden change of feelings from sadness to that of growing excitement at David's presence was a pleasant relief. *This is silly. You'd think I was a teen-ager...but he is pretty special.*

They reached the parking lot just as a slim, dignified man was getting out of a car parked adjacent to hers. *What a pleasant day this had turned out to be after all,* Abby thought as she waved to her brother, Stephen. Stephen was the oldest of the three children of Peter and Dorcas Demitt, and at thirty was firmly entrenched in the financial world of New York as an advisor to a number of wealthy clients. Stephen was tall and lean with dark hair cropped in the latest fashion for the affluent New York businessman.

He made the short trip back to Vesta often, especially since the death of their parents. Although he insisted his trips were to make sure his baby sister was doing well, Abby had a feeling that might have been an excuse for him to briefly get away from the stress he encountered in New York and the stress that seemed to be building in his marriage.

Stephen had met his wife Tiffany at a ritzy party in New York at the home of one of his clients. He fell for her immediately and soon talked her into marriage. Although there were many ups and downs in their married life, the arrival of their twin boys seemed to be a healthy event for their relationship.

"Hi, Stephen! Where are Tiffany and the twins? Didn't they come with you?" Abby questioned as she let go of Josh and David and walked quickly to hug her older brother. "I was looking forward to seeing them the next time you were in town…the boys are eight already and I've hardly spent any time with them."

Stephen shook his head as Abby continued, "Tell them I miss them. Maybe you can bring them for dinner sometime. The boys enjoyed exploring the cave in back of the house last time they were here. Tiffany might enjoy a visit too, it's been a long time."

By the time she finished greeting her older brother, she had been thoroughly hugged and was dragging him by the hand to join Josh and David. "You remember David, don't you, Stephen?" she asked as she smiled warmly at the young man who was pleasantly extending his hand.

"Yes. How're you doing, David?" Stephen said, shaking David's hand somewhat absently. "Oh, Josh. Thought maybe we could get those traverse rods up for Abby while I'm here."

"But, aren't you going up to the grave?" Josh asked surprised.

"Oh, been up there already. I came earlier this morning, then went to see a client and drove by again thinking you and Abby just might be here."

"Traverse rods?" Josh remembered his brother's question. He enjoyed helping his sister whenever he could, and it would be even more fun now with Stephen here. "Well…sure, I guess we could help out our baby sister. What about you, David? Want to join us?"

David was about to accept the invitation until he glanced at Stephen who obviously didn't like Josh's idea. Stephen had always been an over-protective brother, and since their parents had died he seemed to have taken on the role of her unsolicited guardian.

"Ah, thanks anyway. I've got some things to take care of, but I would like to borrow Abby for a minute before I leave." With that he extended his arm to her and they walked ahead down the path.

He smiled. "I've wanted to ask you out since I've been back but the timing wasn't right. By any chance would you be interested in hearing that new jazz band at the Vesta Square tonight …?"

Abby tried not to show too much enthusiasm as she answered slowly. "Well…I guess that would be all right. I mean…sure, I'd love to go." Jazz was one of the special music treats she allowed herself to enjoy in her busy world, and the prospect of sharing top jazz artistry with David was truly compelling.

David tried to hide his growing attraction for her as he smiled and made plans to pick her up at 8:00. Little did he realize that this evening would be the beginning of a loving but traumatic journey ahead for both of them.

Stephen and Josh were following behind and had almost reached them as David winked at Abigail and made his farewells, heading back to his car. Abigail watched him until his car was out of sight and then turned back to see her brothers both observing her intently. Josh was smiling, but Stephen was quite expressionless.

"Come on over to the house. I'll put on some coffee while you two take care of my traverse rods," Abigail lovingly chided as she got in her car and left the cemetery with her brothers following.

Chapter Two

Abigail's house was nestled in a wooded area at the end of Davis Cave Road, aptly named for the Davis family who years before had discovered the cave at the back of their property. The cave had intrigued Abigail the first time she spotted it. It was almost hidden in the forested grotto behind the house. The mysterious cave seemed to beckon to her beyond the back yard which was filled with wildflowers and interesting rock formations.

It had only taken an afternoon to decide this was *the* house. It would be her Hansel and Gretel-style house with its enchanting curved roof and flowering window boxes that brought to mind the fairytale of long ago. That would have been enough to get her attention, but upon entering the house, Abigail just *knew*.

The great room engulfed her with its warmth. At one end was a fireplace with a hand-carved mantle and various hues of split rock extending to the open beam ceiling. On either side of the rock were massive windows overlooking the wildflowers in the back yard and just beyond that a view of the enchanting old cave.

After the sadness of the cemetery, Abby was happy to open the door for her brothers. The smell of fresh cookies that Abby had baked earlier in the day warmed their moods.

"Come on into the kitchen and I'll put on the coffee. I don't suppose either of you would like some special monster cookies?" Abigail said, smiling. Her brothers each made a dash for the kitchen to reach the cookies, and memories flooded her mind of the early years when the boys tripped over each other to get the cookies their mother had baked. Memories upon memories. *I wish there weren't always shadows surrounding the memories,* Abby thought, as she set the cookies at equal distance between the brothers.

Josh hungrily devoured several cookies but stopped long enough to inquire, "Talked to Sarah lately, Abby?"

Stephen nodded, "Yah, Sis. How is she doing anyway? Haven't seen her for a couple of months and I really feel guilty about it."

Abigail took a breath before answering, trying to be honest and yet hating to relay fears of how Sarah was aging. "I took lunch over to her at the home yesterday. She is still extremely alert for her age and that hasn't changed, but she's slowed down a lot and just isn't able to move about nearly as much." Tears came to her eyes thinking of the woman who had been a grandmother to them throughout the years, and now since their parents' death had become just about their entire family.

"Sarah's always been there for us, hasn't she?" Josh said gazing into space. "I remember when she came to live with us, don't you guys?"

"Sure do," said Stephen. "It was after that awful time…"

At those words Abigail perked up. "Hey, guys, when are you ever going to tell me the details about that? You always tell me you can't remember, but sometimes I wonder," Abigail said, her voice rising. "It's like you've always had a secret from me, and even Sarah never offers much information. She just gets a sad look and changes the subject."

"What I remember of that nightmare," affirmed Josh "is that our whole family was held like prisoners in that awful old warehouse. Then Mom had to leave with you, Abby, and Stephen, Dad and I were left there."

"That's when Sarah came into the picture," Stephen added, getting caught up in the nostalgia. "Remember that deal with the ceiling vents, Josh? Boy, that was really hard for me to do, but it did help Sarah get an idea how to help us escape. Wow...such a long time ago," Stephen's voice trailed off.

"You've told me some of that before," Abigail added, "about how you climbed up into the ductwork through the ceiling vent to make out some kind of map for Sarah, but *why* were we all there? What reason could there have been to lock up our whole family? Come on, guys. Please, please tell me what you know!"

Stephen looked intently at Josh and Josh nodded, answering, "We don't remember many of the details, Abby, and we honestly don't know *why* we were all held there."

"It's really a genuine mystery," added Stephen. "I think the reason we've been hesitant to tell you much about it, Abby, is that Josh and I always felt it had something to do with you and your adoption. I overheard Mom and Dad talking during that time. Mom said that nobody was ever going to take you away from us."

"Really?" said Abigail loudly. "I wonder what she meant by that. Who would ever do that anyway? My only recollection of that time is a trip on a plane. Oh...and I do remember that lady with the beautiful red hair. It's all very strange, and whenever I asked Mom anything about it, she'd say we'd talk about it later...but unfortunately, later never came...and now they're gone."

The conversation was getting interesting but bittersweet when they were interrupted by the shrill ring of the phone on the counter next to Abigail. She smiled as she heard David's voice on the line and actually blushed. "Dinner before? Oh, that sounds great," Abigail replied, trying to curb the excitement in her voice. "Seven would be fine. See you then."

"That David again?" Stephen asked almost rudely. "When did all this start?"

"What's the matter, Stephen?" Abigail asked in a hurt voice. "Why don't you like David? After all, he's a good friend of your own brother. I've always liked him and I hope I'll be seeing lots more of him."

"Yes, what *is* your problem with him, Stephen?" Josh said defending his good friend.

"Hey, I'm sorry, Abby," Stephen said apologetically. "I just hate to think of you going out with *any* guy these days. Seems like they're all out for a good time, and you deserve the best."

"Well…thanks, I guess," Abigail said as she glanced quizzically at Josh. "Just remember that I am a pretty good judge of people, Stephen, and trust me. OK?"

Stephen smiled and grabbed her hand. Josh looked intently at his brother and in his best Sunday voice said, "Don't forget God is watching over her."

Stephen frowned, cleared his throat and quickly changed the subject. "Getting back to that mysterious time years ago, I wonder if Sarah remembers much about it. Did she ever talk to you about it, Josh?"

Josh shook his head, and then suddenly blurted out, "Stephen. Remember that first time that Sarah came to see us after we were finally back home safe and she was all beat up?"

As Stephen nodded, a look of recollection crossed his face. "Yes. I remember. And I remember she had a file of some kind that she was very secretive about as she handed it to Mom and Dad."

Josh moved his chair up to the kitchen table ready to share in the fresh remembrances of that time twenty-years ago. "Yes. Now it's clearer. I remember Dad nodding his head when Sarah gave him the file as if he knew already what was in it. Then he quickly took it and filed it in his office somewhere. I don't know what ever happened to it, and with all the excitement of having Sarah with us, I never thought about it much again."

"OK, Fellas. Now just what are you thinking anyway? Any idea what the infamous file contained?" Abigail questioned, trying to sound lighthearted. But as she glanced from one brother to the other, she saw they were quite serious.

"Where do you suppose that file is, Josh?" Stephen said as he started making notes on a pad. "I'll bet Sarah knows, or at least has a good idea."

"You know, I was just thinking the same thing," Josh confirmed. Then looking at his sister who was sitting beside them wide-eyed, he continued. "Abby, you're especially close to Sarah. Do you think you can get any information from her about the location of that file? Maybe she'd even tell you what's in it."

By this time Abby was fully engrossed in the subject and was as curious as her brothers, not only about the file but about the whole episode that took place when she was only two-years-old. Then something Stephen had said earlier began filtering through her mind...*I think the reason we've been hesitant to tell you much about it, Abby, is that Josh and I always felt it had something to do with you and your adoption.* She shook her head vigorously to get rid of the thought as if avoiding a pesky fly, but it didn't take away the uneasy feeling growing in her mind. *First Mom and Dad having to discuss something about my adoption on that dreadful night a year ago, and now I hear other news about my adoption from my brothers. It's terribly strange.*

Then, focusing again she asked, "What was it you asked me? I'm sorry I got to thinking and forgot it. Oh, that's right. You wanted to know if I would talk to Sarah and see if she would give me any information…sure, I suppose."

"Abby. Just let us know if she tells you anything," Josh said, looking with concern at his sister. "Don't let it get to you though…remember, it was a long time ago."

Stephen rose from the table, motioning to Josh. "We'd better get going on those traverse rods so we can get out of here and let Abby get ready for her date."

Later as the brothers finished their task, Stephen said enthusiastically, "This has been great, guys. Let's plan to have dinner together somewhere in a couple weeks when I get into town and I'll see if Tiffany and the twins can come."

Abby watched her brothers walk down the sidewalk as they left. They were so precious to her. *What fun we always had growing up*, she thought nostalgically. *I do remember when we were all safe at home after being separated for awhile. It was so special to be snug in our home again. Even as a little girl I can remember knowing that God was with us.*

"Stephen was happy then," Abigail reminisced out loud. "Somehow over the years his search for success seemed to have taken a lot of his happiness and faith away. Even Josh, the inspired preacher he is, can't seem to talk to him about it."

She waved through the window at the departing cars, and then checking her watch she realized there was only an hour left before David would come. *David,* she thought with a delightful shiver. Then heading for the bedroom and her shower, she determined the questions still confronting her about the past would not ruin her most special evening.

Chapter Three

The evening was special...in fact, for both Abigail and David it was magical. Dinner at La Maison was an occasion to be remembered, and both of them delighted in the quiet charm and delectable cuisine. By the time they ate their dessert, it was obvious they had become even more delighted in each other. Abby knew it was not an ordinary date on an ordinary night...it was the beginning of something extraordinary. She glanced at David's face and knew without a doubt that it was the beginning of something special for him as well.

As they walked out of the restaurant David grabbed her hand and squeezed it warmly and Abby squeezed back. At that moment if anyone would have asked what they had for dinner, neither would have remembered.

Is this how it starts? Abby wondered. *How can I even think of love...this is our first date.* But, somewhere in the recesses of her mind, Abby knew. She just knew.

Later, as the young couple sat holding hands and smiling at each other listening to jazz music provide their romantic background; Josh and Stephen sat in Josh's apartment located above the Community Christian Church garage. Stephen gratefully accepted a hot cup of coffee from his brother and eased himself into Josh's huge leather chair.

"That's my thinking chair," Josh said. "I do my best work there."

Stephen looked up at the younger brother he admired and often wished that he could emulate. "Well, I wish I had a thinking chair...one that would actually do the thinking for me. Sometimes I have no idea what to do about my life."

Josh sat down quietly on the chair next to him. He had been concerned about his brother for some time, and now maybe he would be able to find out how he might help him.

"What is it, Stephen?" Josh asked, trying not to sound too much like a preacher. "Is it anything you'd like to talk over? You seem so discouraged."

Stephen wasn't one to talk about his personal feelings, but his situation with Tiffany had reached the point where he didn't know what to do. Maybe his brother could actually give him some advice...or encouragement...or something.

"Josh, my marriage isn't right, possibly my parenting isn't right, and sometimes I even wonder if I'm handling my job right. And I'm too young for male menopause."

Josh tried to keep the conversation on a lighter note. "Hey, I hope you're too young. You're only two years older than I am...and I can tell you I'm not ready to wonder where my life went."

"I don't know, Josh," Stephen said, ignoring his brother's attempt at humor. "Tiffany and I just seem to be going separate ways, and the boys are caught between. It breaks my heart, but whenever I try to talk to her about it, it just ends up in a fight."

Josh got up and went into the kitchen for the coffee carafe, saying over his shoulder, "Want to spend the night and we can talk?"

Stephen looked up with a glimmer of hope that was somehow mixed with despair. "I guess I could, but don't give me any lectures about God in my life, OK?"

As Josh refilled his brother's cup, he thought about the faith the two of them had shared as boys. *In fact, it was at the time of the family's ordeal in that awful warehouse that Stephen and I first opened our hearts to a faith in Jesus,* Josh remembered, smiling. *We shared that faith all through school. When did Stephen give it up?*

Josh took advantage of his brother's quiet mood and tried to determine the time in Stephen's life when his faith didn't mean much to him anymore. *Was it in college? Or, maybe the last year of high school when those kids from that wealthy suburb accepted him into their group? That does seem to be the time of the slow change in him. What was it, striving for success, or striving for the approval of the rich kids?*

Stephen got up slowly, grabbed his cell phone from his jacket and dialed home. When he reached Tiffany, it was obvious from the conversation that she really wasn't concerned whether he came home that night or not.

"Well, that's taken care of," Stephen said bitterly. "My spending the night here isn't going to shake up her world at all."

Josh tried to change the mood and took sandwich fixings from his refrigerator, piling meats and cheeses onto thick pieces of sourdough bread. "Here," he said putting one of the plates on Stephen's lap, "just like Mom used to make for us."

They sat in silence as they devoured the tasty sandwiches and consumed more hot coffee…Stephen thinking about the heavy load he was carrying on his shoulders, and Josh thinking how to begin their talk without being too obvious. He finally decided the best place to start was to go back and reminisce about the family's "adventure," as their mother had referred to it, although no one actually thought of it as an adventure…more like a nightmare.

"Stephen," Josh said, jolting his brother out of his dark thoughts, "talking earlier about the old warehouse and the ceiling vent…that was a *good* memory of a horrible time, wasn't it?"

Stephen perked up and smiled. "When I think about it now, I can't believe I was brave enough to go up into that ceiling vent to get information for Sarah." He chuckled as he continued, "Those lunch trays she brought us with the secret notes telling us how we could help her figure a way out of there for us…they were actually fun, something we had to look forward to in that dismal room. Remember the first time I went up there and came back scared to death? I didn't even go much past 10 or 20 feet."

"I remember being so proud of you I was ready to burst," Josh added to the memory. "Then when you were brave enough to go up there a second time…it was great! You crawled all the way to the end and made a map of the rooms and the direction for Sarah that helped her figure out how to find the secret passage out of that building. You helped get us out of there."

"I still wish I knew why we were all held there and why Mom and Abby had to leave," Stephen reminisced. "If it was all about Abby's adoption, what could have been so different about her adoption that would be important enough to imprison us?"

The question triggered Josh's memory. "About five years ago Sarah started to tell me about where Mom and Abby were sent to…somewhere in Europe near the Mediterranean Sea, but she just stopped suddenly as if she had forgotten she wasn't supposed to say anything. It was all very odd."

Stephen yawned and looked over at the hide-a-bed couch. "Well, maybe Abby will find out something from Sarah. They've always been close." He yawned again. "Any objection to me hitting the sack? I think I've had enough reminiscing for awhile."

Josh knew he had to say one last thing before the conversation ended. "Stephen, do you remember *why* you were able to go up into that ceiling vent the second time?"

"Well sure, you were praying…ah, no God stuff, remember?"

That was all the talk for the night, but as Stephen turned out the light by the couch and Josh turned out the light in his bedroom, Josh prayed for his brother once again.

Chapter Four

Sarah had just turned off her light and snuggled under the covers when the phone rang. *Who in the world would be calling me at this hour of the night? Probably a wrong number.* But, unable to listen to the ringing phone, she reached over and picked up the receiver.

"Sarah! I am so excited and happy I just had to call you. It's wonderful, just wonderful. I can't even explain it. And it happened so fast. I just can't believe it!"

"Abby dear, is that you?" Sarah said, glancing at the clock on her side table. "It's after midnight, Child, are you sure you're all right?"

"Oh, Sarah, I'm more than all right. I'm excited, I'm thrilled, I'm happy, I'm tingling, I'm wonderful…just wonderful."

"What is it, dear? It must be good news? Tell me all about it." Sarah sat up in bed smiling, delighted to hear from her wonderful Abby, no matter what the time.

"Well," Abby began breathlessly, "I had a date with David tonight. You remember, David McNeal, Josh's best friend? He's tall with sandy hair, and what we girls refer to as a real 'hunk.' I used to have such a crush on him. At the time of the funerals we talked, and he was so kind. But I barely remember much that happened other than the funeral. Well, he must have remembered me because yesterday he asked me out for dinner and a jazz concert. Do you believe in love-at-first-sight, Sarah?"

Sarah fumbled on the table for her glasses as if they would help her think. "Well, yes. I guess I do believe in love-at-first-sight. It was somewhat that way with my husband and me. We only dated twice, I think it was, but I knew. I just knew. He must have loved me too because from then on we were inseparable."

"Oh, Sarah. I'm just so happy I could burst, and I had to share it with you ..." Abby chattered on for minutes describing the restaurant, and how David had grabbed her hand, and how they sat listening to the jazz concert but not hearing much because they were so engrossed in each other. Suddenly she stopped. "Oh, please forgive me. I'm chattering on and it's past midnight. I hope you don't mind that I called so late, but you know I share everything with you. I'll stop over sometime this week and let you get a few words in, OK? I love you, Sarah."

Sarah sat upright in bed for a long time after hanging up the phone, smiling with joy at being able to share her precious Abby's happiness…until…she remembered what she had to do. Then the smile faded and her heart beat faster. "How do I do this, Lord, how?"

She pulled back the covers slowly, because at her age she wasn't able to do anything quickly anymore. As she slipped on her warm fleece robe, she hoped the warmth of it would ease some of the arthritic pain that was her constant companion. She grabbed her cane as she headed for her closet. There it was, facing her like an enemy…the lockbox she had kept hidden since Abby's mother had given it to her many years ago.

Once again she questioned herself. *How will I be able to give Abby that file? I don't even want to look at it ever again, but she has to see it. The news might affect her relationship with David, and certainly it'll affect her whole life.*

"Oh, God," Sarah cried. "Help me!"

As Sarah prayed for the strength to reveal the contents of the box to Abby, Abigail was praying with thanks. She was so happy. Even things in her house seemed different…all sparkly and radiant. She danced from the great room into her bedroom just as the phone rang. It was David, calling to say good-night again and tell her he was thinking of her. She shivered at the sound of his voice and had to sit down on the bed to keep her balance.

"Hi," she said lovingly. "I'm thinking of you too. It was the most wonderful night of my life and I thank you." She nodded and smiled as she accepted his invitation to see her the next day for lunch. Thankfully, she didn't have to be on duty at the hospital until Monday morning. As she hung up the phone, she stretched out on her bed happily reviewing the evening and fell asleep without changing clothes or even turning out the light.

Sarah finally fell asleep as well, but her dreams were of the lockbox. It floated through the dreams in various colors and sizes, growing larger and larger until all at once it burst open spilling out papers. Sarah awoke with a start and it took several hours and two aspirins for her to get back to sleep.

The next morning as Sarah began dressing for the day she seemed to have the answer to her cry for help the night before. This week when Abby came for her visit, she'd have to tell her the details of that awful nightmare in her family's life and prepare her for what she would see in the lockbox. Sarah knew it would be the hardest thing she'd ever have to do. *But she has every right to know,* she reasoned. *And every right to know it was this very thing that Abby's mother and father had to tell her the night of her birthday when they traveled through those canyon roads in the rain.*

Dorie's voice sounded so frightened on the phone that night before they left for the party. She and Peter had finally gotten up the nerve to tell their daughter the terrible truth. They couldn't put it off any longer. They were going to help Abby celebrate her 21st birthday, stay overnight and then tell her everything while they were able to be with her.

"It was the last time I ever talked to Dorie," Sarah acknowledged sadly.

I've been putting off telling Abby myself since that time...hoping it would all go away. But, it never will...and Abby must know.

As Sarah tried to plan what she would say to Abby on her next visit, Abby had finished breakfast in her sunny kitchen and headed for the dressing room to get as glamorous as she could for her luncheon with David. Before meeting him at the Crepe House, she wanted to quickly stop at the hospital and look over her mail in preparation for her shift on Monday.

She looked approvingly at her vibrant red hair that hung in loose waves at her shoulders and she began brushing vigorously. As she applied a small amount of eye makeup, her dark blue eyes with their emerald highlights looked back at her, and for a moment she stopped to wonder what her "real" mother had looked like.

Then, dismissing that thought, she concentrated on the wardrobe for her special lunch. She picked out a light blue casual slacks and jacket and found just the right royal blue turtleneck to bring out the color of her eyes. Flat shoes would be best, and she couldn't forget the necklace her mother had given her on her sixteenth birthday. It was a delicate gold cross and a medallion inscribed with the Bible verse, John

3:16. "For God so loved the world, that he gave his only begotten Son, that whosoever believeth in him should not perish, but have everlasting life."

All her mother would tell her about it was that it was given to her by a minister years before, and it was one of her most cherished pieces.

As Abby finished coordinating her ensemble, she looked approvingly in the mirror and left for her exciting day. *Maybe I'll even find time to stop and visit with Sarah this afternoon,* she thought as she locked the door to her Hansel and Gretel house and headed for her car.

Chapter Five

Sarah had gotten a call from Abby telling her she would be over in the afternoon after her date with David. *I need to tell her today,* thought Sarah. *I've put it off much too long, and it's time.* As she walked slowly back and forth in her room, leaning heavily on her cane, she could think of nothing else. Sarah was convinced God helped her make that decision in spite of all the pain that would be sure to follow.

Should I call Josh and Stephen and have them come over to support Abby? Then thinking more rationally she decided against it. "No, I can't do that. Josh and Stephen don't know this either, and it is something Abby should choose to tell them herself." All morning Sarah walked in her room carrying on her quiet conversation.

At Vesta Memorial Hospital Abby finished sorting through the mail and stepped out into the hallway. She was pleased to see that all the nurses were busy and productive. As she watched them answer room calls, prepare meds and contact doctors, she felt so blessed that she had been hired to work with these women who were such gifted nurses.

Abigail had been a top student in college and was skilled in her nursing profession as well as her organizational abilities, which led to her consideration for the job at Vesta Memorial. Though she was a new graduate in the bachelor degree nurses program when she was hired as a staff nurse, she felt confident that she hadn't disappointed her supervisor or the board. She knew her employers respected her abilities, but the respect she received from the other nurses was even more important to her.

After finishing at the hospital, she sped quickly to the Crepe House. As she approached, she scanned the parking lot for David's car and spotted it near the entrance. She pulled into a spot near his just as he stepped out of his car. *Every time I look at him I tingle,* Abby thought as she opened her door. Standing face to face with David as they met, she had to stifle an urge to lean over and kiss him soundly. As she glanced at him, she was sure that was his desire as well.

Lunch was full of warmth and love. They held hands and smiled at each other so long that they became the center of attention.

"David, I never knew I could be this happy," Abby said lovingly, all the while thinking, *I love you, David.*

As if he knew what she was thinking David spoke quietly, "I know it's soon, Abby, but I think I've loved you ever since you used to pester me when I came to see Josh years ago."

Well, that did it for both of them, and the rest of the lunch was a blur of smiles, touching hands and whispered happiness.

The waitress came with their bill though they scarcely remembered paying her as they walked to the door holding hands. A few people gave them nods of approval as they left, and one man even gave them the thumbs-up sign.

"Come with me to meet my dear Sarah," Abby said as they neared her car. "Want to follow me?"

David readily agreed and in minutes was in his car following Abby to the nursing home for his first meeting with Sarah.

The lobby of the Vesta Senior Nursing Facility was busy with activity. Visitors were coming and going, and a group of youngsters from one of the churches was entertaining some of the seniors with songs of the old days. Many of the residents greeted Abby as she held David's hand and walked through the lobby and hallway leading to Sarah's studio apartment.

"Well, here we are David. Beside my brothers and Uncle Don whom you'll meet, Sarah is my entire family and I love her dearly."

Sarah had been waiting anxiously for her to come and appeared at the door the minute she heard the knock. When she opened the door, her smile faded just a bit as she glanced at David standing with Abby. "Oh-h-h-h," she stuttered, "I didn't know you were bringing someone. Please come in."

Abby could scarcely wait to get David into the room before she put her arm around his waist and introduced her *wonderful* David to Sarah. David smiled and warmly grasped Sarah's hand, so genuinely in fact that she melted right on the spot.

"I'm happy to meet you, David. Abby has talked of no one else since your dinner date and the concert." She led him to the sofa and patted the seat next to her. "Please come and sit down and tell me all about yourself."

It seemed to David that this grey-haired woman was a loved one he had known all his life, and as he sat next to her he was able to comfortably relate the details of his life.

"Sarah...may I call you Sarah?" She nodded and smiled encouragingly. "I don't have much of a story. Began high school in Vesta, left to attend college the year my parents became missionaries to South America. After that, law school."

Sarah smiled, observing his expressions and his demeanor.

"Tragically, my parents died about four years ago from a flu epidemic in their village. It was an extremely difficult time for me...they were great parents. They gave me extraordinary memories to hang on to."

David hesitated for a moment to control his emotions.

"Oh, I'm so sorry to hear your parents are dead," Sarah said with genuine concern. "Death can be a terrible thing to face, but I've found there's great comfort found in faith. Did you find God helped you through your grief, David?"

"Yes I did. I don't know what I would have done without that."

Sarah smiled, patted his hand and asked him to continue his story.

"Well, my parents had left enough money for me to finish law school and I graduated recently. I'm now a lawyer with Kent & Kolb right here in Vesta. Everyone in the firm has been very helpful to me and encouraged my pro-bono work on the side."

"I'm glad that you shared your history with me. You seem to be a fine young man. You apparently have handled the traumatic part of your life in a positive way and still been able to count your many blessings. I admire you for that."

Sarah looked over at Abby as if for permission and then asked her leading question. "You said you relied on God during that most difficult time in your life and had faith…are you a Christian, David? I know that's an important part of Abby's life."

"Yes I am, Sarah. My faith in God is an important part of my life too. Actually, I'm a member of Josh's church and work along with him on a number of projects." David looked over at Abby and smiled. As he glanced back at Sarah he saw she had tears in her eyes.

"I'm sorry. Sarah. Did I say something wrong?"

"Oh no," Sarah responded. "I've been praying that Abby would find a young man who could share her faith, and now I know she has."

It was a happy family event as they continued to share stories. Even though Sarah knew she would soon have to tell Abby the most horrendous news of her life, she was able to be in the moment and share Abby's joy with her David.

"Well, I've got to get back to the office and meet a client," David said, "but this has been great…a special afternoon. Getting to know you brings me closer to the memory of my own parents. You're pretty special." David clasped Sarah's hands in his own as he spoke, "I'll look forward to seeing you again soon."

Abby walked with him through the lobby to the door, and their eyes kissed. "Soon," was David's good-bye, and her response as well. As she watched David walk to his car, she had no way of knowing that circumstances would alter her happy plans.

Sarah sat on her couch waiting for Abby to return, and she shivered. This would be unbelievably difficult. Abby was as precious to her as her own child would be, and the thought that she had to tell her such terrible news was devastating.

A quiet little knock and Abby had slipped back in the room, smiling at Sarah with a dream-like expression on her face. "Isn't he wonderful, Sarah?"

"Yes, Abby. I liked him very much, and I'm so glad you two found each other. He'll take good care of you and I'm sure he'll be able to help you through many things."

Abby sat down next to Sarah and looked at her quizzically. "Whatever do you mean, Sarah? He'll help me through *what* things?"

This was it. Sarah could put it off no longer. She reached over for the lockbox the building manager had gotten down for her and opened it as she began the story that would change Abigail Demitt's life forever.

Chapter Six

Sarah reached into the lockbox and withdrew a yellowing file folder.

"What's that?" Abby questioned. "The boys have been talking about a mysterious file, and wanted me to ask you about it. Do you think that's the one they were talking about?"

"Abby, this is confirmation of what I'm going to tell you. But, before getting to what's in this folder, let me start at the beginning.

"The first thing I must tell you is that your mother called me before they left to see you on your birthday…the night they were killed. She and your dad had made up their minds that they were going to tell you the whole story that I am about to tell you. Sadly, they never made it. They would have been able to give you the details first hand and related them to you better than I am able.

"I'll do my best. I'll give you the background of what happened to you and your family all those years ago, and will try to help you though it all. It's an unbelievable story, but let me assure you, it is *true*."

As Abby settled back apprehensively on the couch, a tingling of fear crept through her. "Please go ahead, Sarah. If it's something my parents were going to tell me, I want to know. I do have to admit, though, that I'm somewhat fearful at what you have to say."

Sarah stroked Abby's hair and touched her face lovingly, closed her eyes for strength and then began.

"Of course, you know your mother and father adopted you from the Montgomery Agency when you were three months old. They loved you so much and your older brothers idolized you." Abby nodded and smiled, encouraging Sarah to go on.

"Well, when you were just about two, your father mysteriously disappeared for four days and your mother was frantic. She called the police and was working with Detective Donovan to find him."

Abby interjected, "You mean Uncle Don?"

"Yes, one in the same. He was a great help to the family then just as he is now. But, getting back to the story. After being gone four days, your father finally called and talked briefly with your mother, telling her he had been kidnapped and driven around in a car before he finally escaped. He had run miles through forests and back roads until he arrived in Watson where he was finally able to contact her."

"Watson…the Watson north of here?" Abby inquired.

"Yes, that Watson. It seems he was running from these two men who had abducted him and were still in pursuit. He eluded them and hid out in the Watson park where he had arranged to meet your mother and you children that night. He made sure she would bring you children because from the bits of conversation he heard in the car, it was apparent you were all in danger.

Your mom and dad finally found each other. They were about to take you children and find a place to plan their next move when the same two men found you all and forced you into their car, taking you to an old warehouse in Deerburn. The boys were locked in a room together, and your mom and dad were in separate locked rooms."

"And me? Where was I?" By this time Abby was sitting upright and rigid as she listened.

"You were being examined by the doctor and his assistant. He was referred to as 'Dr. Nick' and Rhonda was his girl Friday...not nice people at all. Evidently there had been a mistake at the adoption agency and you weren't supposed to be given out for adoption. You were the special baby out of the group of babies. That's basically why they took your family; they were desperate to get you back."

"But why?" Abby asked, near tears.

"That part we'll get into later, all right? First I want to tell you more. I was hired by the doctor along with another nurse to take special care of a baby, and that baby turned out to be you. So, that's where you and I met and I got to love you. I had no idea what the doctor was doing until later just before you and your mother were forced to go overseas to the country of Nortovia with Rhonda, Dr. Nick and his bodyguard, Duke.

There was another woman who also went along. Her name was Ruby, Ruby Cramden, an ex-convict who had become partners with Dr. Nick and Rhonda. She was a key player before, and also in, Nortovia."

Sarah looked over at Abby with concern. "You look like you could use a cup of hot tea. It might relax you a bit."

Abby shook her head and readily encouraged Sarah to go on.

"Well, things didn't work out as the doctor and Rhonda had planned in Nortovia even though Dr. Minolo, their associate there, tried to carry out his part of the bargain. The problem was that Ruby, instead of waiting for Dr. Nick to pay her *after* her work for him was done, demanded the money *beforehand*. Of course, Dr. Nick, being the evil man he was, gave her the run- around so she hatched a plan.

"She had grown quite attached to you and decided she'd really foul everything up for the doctor, plus have you all to herself, if she took you and escaped from him and his bodyguard. So, while your mother was sleeping, she jimmied a window open and fled with you down the fire escape. Your mother woke a few minutes later to discover you were gone.

After searching the suite in panic, she followed through the same window, down the fire escape and out into the street running to find you.

"Well, she found the two of you in a deserted building, but unfortunately Duke, Dr. Nick's henchman, also found the three of you soon after and slammed into the room. He had been instructed by the doctor to get you back under *any* circumstances, and get rid of Ruby and your mother if he had to. A fight started and Ruby actually saved your life by shielding you just as Duke shot her. Even though she was hit, she valiantly fired a shot and wounded him as she fell to the floor."

Abby couldn't wait to ask, "Where was my mother? Was she shot too? What happened?"

"Your mother wasn't hurt, just terrified that something would happen to you. In a way Ruby saved her too by diverting Duke's attention. You see, your mother and Ruby had gotten to be friends and they shared a mutual love for you. After Ruby was shot and Duke lay unconscious, your mother held her in her arms until Ruby cried out to Jesus and slumped over in a heap just as Duke started to regain consciousness. Then your mother took you and ran until the two of you finally ended up in a church with people who took good care of you and shared their faith with her and baptized her. It was a momentous time for your mother, and before the two of you left to get a ride to the airport, the pastor gave her a gold locket with a medallion."

"This must be it," Abby said fondling the locket around her neck. "She gave it to me on my sixteenth birthday, remember?"

Sarah nodded and continued. "Several other harrowing experiences happened to you and your mother before you actually got home safely. Duke tried unsuccessfully to get you, and then you and your mother had to hide from Rhonda who was a threat to your safety as well. She ended up on the same flight back to the States as you and your mother.

"Rhonda had left Nortovia, as we pieced together later, on the pretense that she was going to get things ready back at the lab, but those who knew about the relationship between her and Dr. Nick figured she had revenge on her mind. Although it was apparent she was in love with him, we all thought he was using her until the project they were working on was complete. She must have figured that out and headed to their lab in Deerburn to destroy everything, beginning with the office files at the Montgomery Agency."

"What about Dad and the boys? What happened to them? How did they escape?"

"That's an interesting part of the story," Sarah continued. "I talked to them and your mother through locked doors until you and your mother left. Then I was permitted to bring your father and the boys their meals as long as Sarge, the doctor's guard, was with me each time. He was an evil man, another one of the doctor's henchman, and I was very careful not to do anything to aggravate him.

"Well, your dad and brothers secretly exchanged notes with me on the meal trays. We were trying to work on a plan to help me find the way out of that horrible place so they could escape. Because no phones were available to me and the building was a maze of hidden doors and staircases, escape would have been impossible without Stephen's help. He was the hero."

"Stephen? What did he do? Oh, is that when he helped you find a way out of that place?" Abby said so engrossed in the story that she didn't realize the supper hour had come and gone.

"Stephen twice went up into the ductwork and mapped out the room locations for me so I could figure an escape route by finding out where the door on that floor was hidden. It was during that time that the seeds of faith started growing in each of them and that held them together through their trials."

"What do you mean? How did any faith start in that place?" Abby questioned.

"Well, I had slipped a song sheet with hymns and later a Bible under their door in hopes that they would get a message from it and evidently they did. After I figured an escape route for them, your dad and brothers found their way and once free, got your Dad's friend Tim to come from Vesta to get them. By that time you and your Mom were arriving home and it was a magnificent reunion...a real 'God thing.' Then Detective Donovan helped tie up all the loose ends and life went on."

"Whatever happened to that Ruby? Did they ever find her body?"

Sarah wasn't sure how to answer that question. "Abby, I don't know what to tell you other than the fact that her body was never found. Your mom grieved for her for a long time."

Abby was now leaning forward concentrating on Sarah's every word. Sarah was about to get up and stretch her legs when Abby asked about Rhonda. "Did her plan for revenge ever work out?"

"It seemed like she got her revenge. She had time in the lab to destroy everything she wanted before Dr. Nick and Duke came back. I think the doctor returned out of desperation. He had lost you and then Ruby was shot. I suppose his only hope was to begin another project, but Rhonda must have destroyed any hope he might have had. Then there was that horrific explosion and the whole building was destroyed…with them in it. The police report said it apparently had been caused by a gas leak."

Abby thought for a minute. "But, what about you? How did you escape? I barely remember something about an explosion. We were all together again at our house and watched something on television about a big fire, but it didn't mean anything to me at the time. What really meant so much to me and to our whole family is when you showed up at our door. We were ecstatic. Mom and Dad had been so worried about you. Josh and Stephen said when you came to us you had lots of black and blue marks and seemed to be pretty beat up. Whatever happened?"

Sarah shivered. "That awful guard, Sarge, took it out on me after your Dad and the boys escaped. I was pretty miserable for a day or so but then I remembered the plan your dad and brothers used, and I found my way out of there. It was just then that the doctor and his "buddy" came back from Nortovia. They didn't see me, so I began making my way to the top floor of the building. I had just walked through the door opening to the street level when the explosion rocked the whole area. It was a miracle of God that I made it out safely."

By this time Abby was perched on the edge of the couch and staring intently at Sarah. "I can't believe this whole thing. It's terrible! What an awful thing for you and my family to go through, and all because of that evil man. But, Sarah you haven't told me *why* the doctor was so desperate to get me back! And, what's in that file folder?"

Sarah's eyes filled with tears as she leaned over and hugged Abby with a grandmother's love. She slowly handed Abby the yellowed file and said, "Please remember that I love you, dear, and that this is something you had to know."

Chapter Seven

Abigail Demitt opened the folder and read the first paragraph. She looked up at Sarah in total and absolute disbelief. "This can't be *true,*" she cried out loud. "A HUMAN CLONE? *I'm a clone?* NO…NO! It can't be…it must be a lie, someone made this all up. It's impossible. There are no human clones. Sarah, tell me it's not true. *Please!*" But, as Abby searched Sarah's face, she knew. It wasn't a lie.

At that moment when unbelief turned into the realm of possibility, Abby screamed. Her scream was heard as far as the lobby, jolting the residents. Sarah tried to put her arm around her, but Abby bolted off the couch and headed for the bathroom and was sick.

Sarah quickly picked up the phone with shaking hands and placed a call to Josh's cell phone. Thankfully, Josh picked up on the first ring. "Josh, please come over here right away. Your sister needs you, and I do too."

"Right away," was all Josh could say as he turned his car around and headed to Sarah's senior facility.

As Josh approached Sarah's room he was confronted by a number of residents standing outside her door. He knocked soundly and Sarah came to the door looking much older than he had ever seen her. She ushered him in and then went out into the hall to explain to the crowd of friends that the scream was nothing to be concerned about. Her granddaughter had just had some bad news, but things were all right. It appeared to be enough of an explanation because they soon dispersed, going back to their various activities.

Josh was completely unnerved when he saw his sister. Her skin was a pasty white and her eyes seemed to be glazed over and alarmingly expressionless. She was half sitting and half reclining on the couch, her arm drooping at her side as if she was comatose. He ran to her side and smoothed her hair, speaking slowly and lovingly to her.

When Sarah returned he looked at her for an explanation, but instead of speaking, she walked over to Abby. "Abby, dear. Is it all right for Josh to look at the folder?" Abby looked directly at her brother and some recognition registered as she whimpered, "Josh ..." As if in a trance she handed him the folder and slumped back on the couch. Her eyes didn't move, and she didn't speak. Josh grabbed the folder and glanced at Sarah who nodded approval as tears streamed down her cheeks.

"Oh, my dear Lord! My dear Lord in heaven! This can't be true. Tell me, Sarah, it's not true, is it?" Josh's words had come rushing out in agonizing tones as he saw the horrific words, *human clone.* Abby remained motionless on the couch as if she heard nothing.

Sarah finally spoke. "Josh, it was time for Abby to know. She has a right to know her origin. I explained the whole story of your family's ordeal so she would have some background before I let her see the folder. She reacted so hysterically that I wanted you here so we could figure out what to do. Do you think we should get her to the hospital?"

Josh nodded emphatically and called 911 with instructions to be as discreet as possible when coming through the lobby of the senior facility. He gave Sarah a warm hug affirming her decision and then sat quietly on the floor by his sister gently stoking her arm.

The third floor of the hospital was unusually quiet as the gurney was pushed from the ER to the assigned room.

Sarah held on to one end of the gurney as if to make sure her Abby would be all right, and Josh helped the attendant guide the gurney into Room 310. Abby's initial exam by a resident in Emergency concluded she was in shock and should be kept for observation.

The ride to the hospital had been unnerving for Josh following the ambulance carrying his sister and then listening to Sarah's narration of the trauma his family had gone through when he was just a boy. He was so upset that he almost forgot to call Stephen with the news but finally remembered just as they were pulling into the hospital parking lot.

Now, standing in her room he looked at her seemingly lifeless body and shuddered at the realization of it all. As upset and devastated as he was, he could imagine what it was doing to Abby. How would she be able to handle this? How would *any of them* be able to handle this?

Abby had always been a strong person. Even when their parents died, she relied on her faith in God to get her through. But this, this was something so totally unbelievable that it was impossible to comprehend. As a minister he should be able to say something comforting to his sister, but nothing came. He had nothing for a situation like this, and as far as he knew, no one did.

The resident was taking Abby's blood pressure and checking her eyes as a young nurse adjusted the bedding. Josh glanced at Sarah as if to tell her not to say anything to anyone about the cause of Abby's condition, and she nodded her head ever so slightly.

The young doctor glanced over his horned-rimmed glasses and motioned for Josh to follow him to the back of the room. "Isn't this Abigail Demitt, one of our nurses on this floor? What in the world happened?"

Josh nodded as he struggled to give the doctor some kind of explanation. "It's Abigail. She's my sister. We aren't sure what happened. All we know is that she received some kind of terrible news and she wasn't able to cope with it."

"Well," the doctor answered quickly, "if that's the case, maybe we should try to discover what it was that upset her. Then once we get her stabilized we can have our hospital psychiatrist see her. Do you think the older lady with you might know something that could help?"

"NO!" Josh blurted out without thinking. "I'm sure she doesn't, and I certainly don't want to upset her. She's our grandmother and she's in her eighties. This whole thing has shaken her up quite a bit. Let me talk to her after she calms down a little and see if she has any idea what may have caused Abby's condition."

"I'll leave that to you for now," the doctor said. "Miss Demitt's basics are good, although her heart rate is quite elevated. That's to be expected with the apparent shock that she's had. Right now rest is probably the most healing prognosis, but we'll be checking on her regularly for the next several hours. If you find out something that you think will help us, have the nurse buzz me. I'm Doctor Carlson. In the meantime, I'll give our psychiatrist, Dr. Moore, a call and ask him to see her when it's appropriate."

Josh stepped closer to the bed as the young attractive nurse smoothed Abby's hair. He took a second look at her pixie-like appearance and her short brown hair that curled around her face and was briefly reminded of pictures of his mother when she was young. He noticed she had a tear running down her cheek and he asked if she was all right. "Oh...yes," she replied, "I'm Cindy, and I work with Abigail on the floor. I think the world of her. I just hate to see her like this."

Abby murmured and suddenly sat bolt upright grabbing at Josh's arm frantically. "No! No! No!" It was all she was able to say before falling back down on her pillow. Her eyes were wide and she stared at Josh in panic at the recollection of her nightmare. "Why, Josh? Why?"

"Cindy, would you excuse us, please? I need to talk to my sister. I'll be sure to call if she needs you."

Cindy patted Abby's hand. "I'll be close at hand if you need me, Abigail. I want to help you all I can." As she left the room, Josh was aware the nurse tried unsuccessfully to stifle a sob and then headed quickly down the hall.

"Abby, I don't know *why.* I wish, no I pray, that I did. All I know now is that you're my sister, and no matter what, you always will be. *Nothing* can change that ever. I've called Stephen and he'll be here soon. Between us, we'll see if we can come up with any answers. You just try to hang on."

Sarah got up from the chair she had slumped into minutes before, and stood by the bedside with Josh. She spoke in the reassuring tone that was so familiar to all her loved ones. "Abby, honey, you know we love you with all our hearts. That will never, ever change. Always remember that!" Sarah turned quickly as the tears began to flow, and indicated to Josh that she would step into the hallway.

Within a couple hours Josh heard Stephen's voice asking the nurses for directions and then heard his long strides coming down the hall to Room 310. He greeted Sarah outside the door and then burst into the room breathless, as he managed to say, "Whaaaaat happened? Is she all right?"

He ran to Abby's side and embraced her. "My dear Sis." His tears mixed with his sister's tears and he finally looked up and whispered to Josh, "What happened, Josh? Why is she like this?"

Josh watched as Abby reached up and touched Stephen's face, reassuring herself he was really there. Shortly after, Josh quietly led Stephen to the corner of the room. "I'll ask the nurse to stay with Abby for a few minutes. We need to talk privately. Sarah will come in later, but right now I think she should rest. One of the nurses will show Sarah to a guest room. This has been extremely hard on her as well."

"Yah. Let's talk." Stephen nodded as he followed Josh out the door.

Josh found Cindy in the hallway and asked if she'd find them a private room where they wouldn't be disturbed for awhile. She was more than happy to accommodate him, and soon the two brothers were deep in conversation.

At first Stephen was glad to finally know the details of their nightmarish experience twenty years earlier, but as Josh continued with the horrendous news Abby had just learned that afternoon, Stephen sat listening in horrified silence. His sister a *clone,* a *clone*! It wasn't possible. She is so normal, so beautiful. *It isn't true,* he thought as things bounced around in his head. *There has to be some mistake. People can't be cloned, can they? Wouldn't mom and dad have known?*

"This can't be...there's got to be some mistake," were the only words Stephen managed to say coherently.

The tears washed down Stephen's face, and Josh turned away to give his brother a private moment. He had never seen Stephen unravel like this. Josh, who was still trying to grasp the totality of his sister's cloning, had secretly hoped his older brother would maintain his usual calm and be strong for all of them. But for now that was not to be as Stephen wept silently in his chair, unable to speak.

A quiet tap on the door brought the brothers to attention. Stephen quickly wiped away his tears as Josh walked to the door. Cindy, Abby's nurse, whispered in hushed tones to Josh that Abigail had asked for them. As Stephen rushed out of the room, Cindy turned to Josh, "Pastor Demitt, a gentleman named David has been calling every ten minutes or so to talk to you about your sister's condition. He said you had called him and told him she was here. He asked me to have you call him as soon as possible."

"Ah, David...yes, I'll call him. Thank you, Cindy, you've been a real help." Josh stepped quickly to the nurses' desk to call David as Cindy watched his every move, uttering a silent sigh as she turned to answer a patient light down the hall.

When she returned to the desk she noticed Josh still in conversation, his face contorted in a sadness she had never seen in anyone before. He spoke inaudibly into the phone, ending the conversation. He replaced the phone and walked like a robot down the hall to his sister's room.

David slowly turned his chair toward the window and motioned for his secretary to give him some privacy. The conversation with Josh had only taken a few minutes, but the more he thought of it, the more he realized he hadn't gotten any real information. *How did Josh say it?* David reviewed the conversation in his mind. *Abby had some kind of traumatic news that left her incapacitated for awhile. What news could do that to her?* David stroked his chin nervously. *I want to be with her, but Josh didn't say I should come...or even that Abby wanted me there. What'll I do?*

It didn't take long for David to make a decision. Within minutes he had his coat over his arm, walked out of his office with instructions he would be gone the rest of the day, and headed his car toward the hospital.

Abby was sitting upright looking absently into space when Stephen burst into the room. "Abby! Abby! I can't *believe it.*" But as Stephen sensed her growing panic, he quickly added, "Oh, Sis. I love you so much. Nothing, *nothing* will ever change that. No matter what, you'll always be my little Abby!" And with that he rested his head on her lap and wept again.

Abby reached over touching his hair as she choked out the words, "God help us get through this nightmare!"

Josh returned and the next hour was one of silence as Stephen sat on one side of Abby's bed holding her hand and Josh on the other. No words passed between them. Each was in a separate world fighting off hopelessness.

The silence was broken as Cindy carefully opened the door to explain that a man named David was waiting at the nurses' desk, very anxious to see Abby.

Abby's body began to shake involuntarily and her face turned an ashen grey. "Oh, NO, I can't see him. Tell him I'm sleeping or something, but don't let him see me. Please."

Josh got up from his chair and looked at his sister. "Are you *sure* that's what you want? I know David loves you and must be terribly concerned about you."

"He can't know...can't know...ever! Because I'm a freak, I will *never* be able to see David again."

Stephen jumped out of his chair to embrace Abby. "You're no freak, Sis. You're the same wonderful girl you've always been. Don't say such terrible things about yourself."

Josh took the nurse by the arm and slowly walked down the hall to the nurses' station. "Cindy, I'm asking you as a professional and as my sister's friend to keep everything you hear in that room strictly confidential. It's a matter of grave importance. May I have your word on it?"

Cindy looked up at Josh and was so concerned at the sadness in his face that she almost forgot what he had asked her. "Confidential…of course, Pastor Demitt, I wouldn't think of saying anything. Please believe me." Josh only had a moment to smile at her before spotting David impatiently pacing the floor just ahead of him.

David began to run toward Josh until Josh put his hand up to indicate they would be going into a conference room to talk. "This way, David." Josh took David by the arm and guided him into the room he and Stephen had left a short time before.

"What is it, Josh? What's going on? I love Abby so much; don't I have a right to know how she is?" David was near panic as he did his best to speak without yelling. "You really didn't give me any information other than she had had some traumatic news that she couldn't handle."

By now David's hands were shaking and any courtroom demeanor he possessed became more like one of the frightened clients he defended. Josh and David talked for over half an hour without touching on the actual news that Abigail had learned. Josh finally closed the conversation with words David had feared he might hear.

"David, I know that Abby loves you with all her heart, but right now she insists on managing this news by herself. She says she doesn't want to see you, but I think that's only because she feels at such a loss now about how to handle this. I'm sure this will all be resolved in time, but I do ask if you truly love her, please give her space and try to be patient. I really feel she'll come around."

David put on his coat in robot-like motions and then wiped his face. "You're a great friend, Josh. I appreciate your candor and I will try to be patient. Abby is the only girl I've ever loved and I just can't lose her. Will you please, please tell her I love her and I will wait for her no matter how long it takes? ...Thanks." As they shook hands they knew instinctively that they not only shared a bond of friendship, but also shared a bond of sorrow that couldn't be expressed in words.

Chapter Eight

Abby wasn't able to get her thoughts to flow in any kind of rational form, so she hardly noticed when Josh returned and her brothers took Sarah in the hall to talk privately.

Questions plagued her. *Is all this really true? How could I be a clone...I feel normal and live normally. I can't believe it! I just can't believe it...my life is in shambles.*

How can I ever tell David? I love him so much. But if he knows I'm a clone, the news would make him hate me, or look at me like I'm a freak. How could he love me if he knew? And even if by some unbelievable chance he did find out and would still love me, can someone like me even think about marriage and babies?

Then shaking her head violently as if to rid herself of those thoughts as she often did when thinking unpleasant things, the words she read in that file still reverberated through her mind. *It must be true. Those words were written by the very doctor who cloned...did the cloning.*

So, if I truly am a clone, then I'm not a real person, am I? And if I'm not a real person what about my faith in Jesus that has been my hope all these years? Does that even matter anymore? Abby groaned out loud into the empty room as her fearful thoughts continued. *What about heaven? Do I even have a soul? Maybe even Josh couldn't answer those questions, and if he couldn't answer them as a pastor, who could?*

"Oh, dear God! Oh, God! Oh, God," Abby screamed, but no sound came.

Suddenly, there it was...the question that had been hidden in the recesses of her mind...the question she hadn't been able to think of before...but one that had to be answered.

Who was I cloned from? Hearing that awful news was so devastating that I never asked Sarah. Who was it? Who??

Her disturbing thoughts were interrupted as Cindy came in to check on her and bring a tray of hot tea and broth. "Abby, would you please try to get some of this down? It'll help you, I'm sure." When Abby didn't object Cindy carefully placed the tray on her lap. "Just one more thing…your brother Josh asked me to tell you that he and your brother Stephen are getting something to eat in the cafeteria and they'll be back shortly."

Abby nodded mechanically and then sat staring at the tea. Soon after Cindy left, there was a timid knock on her door. Sarah entered slowly, her eighty-five years more evident than ever. Sarah's eyes were red and swollen from her tears.

"Oh, my dear child," Sarah murmured quietly, "I wish I wouldn't have had to give you such horrendous news, but you had to know."

Abby reached for Sarah's hand as she slumped back into the pillows. Her body involuntarily shook and her sobs were the most sorrowful Sarah had ever heard. Then whispered between the sobs Sarah made out the words, "Who was it? Who was I cloned from? Who, Sarah, who?"

Sarah stood up next to the bed and smoothed Abby's hair the way she had over the years every time Abby had a problem. She leaned over near Abby's ear and whispered, "It was Ruby, dear. It was Ruby you were cloned from, the woman who grew to love you so much."

Several hours crept by and Abby slowly calmed as Sarah sat beside her bed praying. Josh and Stephen returned and sat in the back of the room ready to be of help, if needed.

Sarah glanced often at Abby and was encouraged to see that a bit of color was beginning to return to her face. She gently touched Abby's hand, and to her surprise Abby responded by grabbing her hand tightly as she rested on her pillow and finally let sleep overtake her.

Before dawn Abby awoke. Her stomach was in knots, but there were signs of returning normalcy. Her brothers were gone and Sarah was dozing in the chair beside the bed. Abby turned her head to look at the loving woman who had come to mean so much to her.

"Sarah," Abby whispered softly as the older woman woke. She moved her chair closer to the bed. "Sarah, while I slept I had dreams…strange dreams. Some of them were about that woman…Ruby."

Sarah wasn't sure how to respond. "Abby. You remember I told you before you went to sleep that it was Ruby whose DNA was used to clone you. Well, your mother told me how very much Ruby loved you; so much in fact that she saved your life by shielding you from Duke, even after she was shot. Your mother said that Ruby wanted you with her always and that's the biggest reason she took you with her when she left the hotel room in Nortovia."

Sarah leaned forward and continued, "I don't know if I told you but Ruby stole that file from the agency's office and hid it in her room at her apartment house. She wanted to make sure your family had the file if anything happened to her, so she gave me a note with instructions as to where she had hidden it. When I heard she had been shot I found her note and got the file. I gave it to your mother and father when I came to live with you. The file has been kept in that box all these years. So you see, Ruby did love you. She tried to protect you, and she even shielded you from Duke."

Abby's voice trembled. "How could she love me? How could anyone love me really? I'm just a piece of manufactured flesh, aren't I? I don't even know if I have a soul or a normal human brain, or anything human ..."

Sarah grimaced at Abby's disheartened description, and clutched the side of the bed to regain some composure. "My dear child, everyone who knows you loves you. Your mother and father learned all about your history, yet they loved you to the very end. You were their precious daughter and they literally fought all odds to keep you. Please don't ever think of yourself as being abnormal. However you were formed, you were formed a living, breathing person. Don't ever forget that."

Abby prodded Sarah again, "Tell me more about... Ruby..."

Sarah continued slowly, "Ruby. Ruby Cramden was her name. She was raised in an unhappy home where the father drank and was unfaithful to her mother. He left when Ruby was young and by the time Ruby was in high school, her mother died and Ruby was alone on the streets.

"I guess she thought she was in love with an older man who pretended to love her but who just took advantage of her and trained her to break into places so he'd get money. Well, then she got caught, spent some time in prison, but soon as she got out she went right back into the "business" for herself. Such a sad thing...she thought it was the only thing she was good at. Of course, the next time she got caught she was sentenced to a longer term, and it was in prison that Dr. Nick found her and used her for his cloning experiment."

Abby wiped away a tear. "It seems surreal to think of that same Ruby as the one the doctor used to...*clone*...me. I wish I had known her...it's hard for me to even believe any of this horrible mess."

Sarah sighed and continued, hoping she could make it short and save Abby any more hurt. "Ruby didn't know why the doctor wanted her blood and skin tissue when he and Rhonda came to the prison and met her. She didn't find that out until she got out of prison and went to the Montgomery Agency looking for Dr. Nick and the money they owed her.

"She was suspicious of the woman at the agency and broke into her office at night. Ruby found the file with her name on it and it was there she found out they had used her. That miserable doctor had planned to use her at the time of the big announcement of his successful human cloning, but she got out of prison early and they had to talk her into being a *member* of the team. I guess they figured they could con her out of the money that way."

Sarah looked at Abby's sorrowful expression. "Abby, don't judge Ruby. She was a good woman at heart, and she grew to love you as her very own child. Always remember, she saved you, so don't misjudge her. She truly loved you."

It was a lot of information for Abby to grasp in a short time. Sarah had answered some things for her and yet there were holes in the story that she had to find out. When Sarah had finished, Abby tried to organize her thoughts. She looked intently at Sarah and began hesitantly, "I just can't go on knowing what I know now unless I find some answers about my past."

"What answers are you looking for, Abby?" Sarah questioned, even though she had a good idea what Abby would say.

Abby massaged her forehead as if she had a headache. "Answers to questions about the people who did this…questions about my relationship to God as a *c-l-o-n-e*…and answers to help me figure out just what, or who, I am. Things like that, Sarah. You understand, don't you?"

"Of course I do, Abby dear, but you will wait until you're better physically, won't you?"

Abby didn't want to deceive Sarah, but she knew this was something she needed to do now. She was convinced that the longer she waited for answers, the worse things would become. *Some things have to be done as soon as possible.*

Without answering Sarah's question, Abby changed the subject. "Maybe I'll find someone who can help me know how to get started. Do you think Uncle Don would be a good person to talk to? He might know if Ruby's father is still living, or if there's someone from that Montgomery Agency I could find to talk to, or maybe even someone in that foreign country. I'd like to know you will be OK with this if I choose to do it."

"You know I'll always be behind you. It's the thought of you going out on your own that scares me more than anything. You've just had a severe shock to your system, and you're already suffering...maybe your discoveries will cause even more pain for you. Are you sure you want to risk it?"

For some reason as Abby listened to Sarah's words, she just knew in her heart that she didn't have a choice. For her own mental health she had to take any risk.

Sarah knew Abby so well that she knew there would be no changing her mind. Stephen and Josh were going to take Sarah back to her apartment so she could get more rest and then come back to the hospital to stay with Abby. As Sarah was about to leave, she leaned over with outstretched arms and silently embraced the young woman who would always be her granddaughter, no matter what her background. Then she turned abruptly so Abby couldn't see the tears, and left to find Stephen and Josh.

Abby knew the hospital staff would try to keep her hospitalized for awhile, but her desire to find out something…anything…about her background convinced her she had the physical and emotional stamina to begin her search. As she stood beside her bed for the first time since being admitted, she was weak and had to grasp the bedclothes so she wouldn't fall. But, by the time she reached the closet she appeared to be managing much better.

She put on the clothes she had worn when they brought her…the clothes she had picked out so carefully for her special lunch with David that fateful afternoon, and she wept audibly at the thought of lost love. *Oh, David. We could have been so happy…but, no more.* It was all over and she couldn't let herself think of it again. She wiped her eyes, grabbed her purse and glanced carefully into the hallway, relieved to see it was deserted. Only Cindy was working on charts at the nurses' desk near the elevators, but no one else was in sight for the moment.

Taking advantage of the empty hallway, she edged her way along the wall toward the stairwell. Opening the door, she descended slowly down the stairs hanging tightly to the handrail until she reached the main lobby, and there made her way to the front door and eased her way out. Once outside she fumbled for her cell phone, and soon was in the back of a taxi. She needed to get to Sarah's care facility and get her car from the parking lot without being spotted by her brothers.

Her quest had begun and there was no turning back.

Chapter Nine

Once in her car, she drove quickly to the little house she loved so much. She had to leave town quickly. If Josh or Stephen knew what she was going to do, they'd try to stop her. She took only a moment to gather a few clothes, grab money and her passport and lock the door, wondering when or even *if* she would ever return.

As she sped along in the early morning hours to talk to the one person who might give her help, miles away in the eastern city of Richardson, New York, an old man left the homeless shelter to begin another day of painful hopelessness.

The man made his way through the refuse littering the underbelly of a nearby bridge hoping to find some "treasure" that he could sell for cash. He leaned heavily on a large stick he used for a cane. As he walked, his arthritic legs pained him to the point he had to stop and lean against the bridge wall.

He appeared to be emaciated, his flimsy clothes draped around him in layers, and his face was covered with whiskers dirty from lack of soap and water. The shame and hopelessness of his life was reflected in his sunken eyes, and as he leaned against the bridge, he stared through the morning mist over the water. His thoughts were as cloudy and dark as the river swirling carelessly under the massive structure.

My life's a mess...always been...always will be. My fault too, all my fault. Don't even remember the wife...but that daughter...now, she was somethin'. Wonder what happened to her. She sure hated me...hey, but why not? I loved women, and booze...a lousy father.

Suddenly he was accosted by loud obscenities and running footsteps. Three boys in their early teens ran by him sending papers and garbage shooting out in all directions. One of them turned to look at the old man and laughed cruelly before rejoining his friends in search of a secluded area where they could open the Seagram's they carried.

A police siren echoed in the distance and an unusual fog began to roll in. For a few brief moments the fog covered the layer of filth under the bridge and gave it an ethereal look. His quest of finding something valuable no longer meant much to him and he sat down painfully on a boulder.

Abigail pulled her car into the parking area of Detective Donovan's apartment complex. By the time she reached his door, she was shaking. *It's too early in the morning. I shouldn't have come. But, maybe he won't mind. After all, he must have known all these years about my secret.* Her thoughts were interrupted by the genuinely happy smile on the detective's face as he opened the door.

"Abigail! What a great surprise. Come in…come in, my dear. To what do I owe this unexpected pleasure?" Immediately Abby felt comfortable with this man who had always been a special uncle to her and her brothers. Even though he was well into his seventies, he was always available for them whenever they wanted to talk.

Uncle Don, as she called him, still had the posture and characteristics of a police detective. He stood tall even though he was aging, and possessed a full head of hair which over the last few years had turned completely white. In earlier years women had often tried to get his attention, but he stayed a bachelor. Sarah had once confided to Abby that she felt the detective never married because of his feelings for Abby's mother, Dorcas, or Dorie, as she liked to be called. Dorie had made quite an impression on the detective from the time she first came to him for help to find her husband. In all their continued association he admired her greatly, although no one truly knew just how strong his feelings were.

Abby felt tears come to her eyes as she stood in the doorway. *What a wonderful help Uncle Don has been to our family over the years...and a wonderful friend too. He probably was a special help to Mom and Dad when they were trying to cope with my...cloning. Ugh! I hate that awful word.* That word made her sick to her stomach and she had to stop to take a few deep breaths. She was deep into her nightmare when she suddenly realized her uncle was calling her name.

"Abby? Abby? Are you all right? Come, sit down and tell me why you're here. Is something wrong?"

Well, she thought, *I might as well come right out with it.* "Please forgive me for coming here so early in the morning, but you've always been such a good friend that I hoped you wouldn't mind. 'What's wrong' is that I've just learned *the* most unbelievable, horrible news about myself and I'm having great difficulty even registering it in my mind. You probably know what devastating news I mean?"

The detective led Abby to the couch and then slowly took his place in a nearby chair. As he looked at her, the sadness in his eyes would have been confirmation enough for Abby. "Yes, Dear Child, I know and I would give anything if I could change the situation. Did Sarah tell you?"

Abby nodded as the tears streamed down her cheeks. They both sat quietly for several minutes as if trying to grasp the reality of it. "I completely lost it when she first told me and they had to take me to the hospital. At first I couldn't get a grip...it was so absolutely unbelievable that my mind couldn't function. Finally, though, I got through the shock somehow and determined that if it is true, I have to know all about it...including anyone who might be living who was part of it."

Looking expectantly at the detective she continued, "That's why I came to you. I'm leaving here, for awhile at least, and I'm going to find out who, or what, I am. I thought you might have some names and facts that might help me. Can you tell me *anything*?"

"Are you sure you want to do this, Abby? You might run in to more than you're bargaining for. A number of those people were criminals and anyone associating with them might have criminal instincts as well." But even as he spoke, it was obvious this young woman he had known and loved since she was two years of age, was determined and nothing he could say would change her mind.

"I want to do this...no, I *have* to do this, for my own sanity," Abby responded quickly.

"OK, Abby, I can see I won't be able to change your mind. It's your decision. Let me find my notes. They're probably in a box packed away in my closet somewhere. Just sit and try to relax and I'll be back in a minute."

As he left to find the notes that would start her on her journey, Abby tried to calm herself. She felt as if her nerves were all raw and exposed, grating and rubbing under her skin, and she had the impulse to scream or run. Instead she continued to breathe in and out, in and out...as if taking one step and then another.

When Detective Donovan returned he was carrying an oversized, obviously heavy metal file. Abby jumped up to help him set it on the table and watched as he opened it and located the large expandable file with her name on the cover. "Well, here it is, Abby. I don't want to hide anything from you, so let's look at it together."

As they sat to begin the task, he pointed to a handwritten note on yellowing, aged paper. "Listed here are the only people that were thought to be alive after that terrible fire who were involved in any way with the nightmare your family went through."

Abby looked at the strange names and then glanced inquiringly at the detective. "Who are these people? I'm not familiar with any of the names here."

"Well, Abby, let's start with the one person your mother said was her greatest help while she was in Nortovia. That was, let's see ..." the detective picked up a tabbed page, "oh yes, here it is. It was a Pastor Petrov, the pastor of the Great Redeemer Church in Zenova, the capital city of Nortovia. He might be someone you'd want to contact if you plan to go there at some point. Just remember, that's a long way from Vesta or even from the States."

He looked closely at the next name. "Here's a real bad guy, Abby. Name's Don Westby. He was one of the henchmen hired by Dr. Nick, and as I understand, was one of the two men instrumental in abducting your family from that park in Watson."

Abby sat watching her Uncle Don's facial expressions and was sure just by the look on his face she would have guessed Don Westby was no good.

"Do you think he's still alive?"

"I wish I could answer that, Abby. I do know this gal Trudy Smithson, the next name here on the list, was the woman who came to the house with Westby and tried to deceive your mother into letting them take you for further tests. I heard she died of some disease a few years ago. That visit was the first attempt to get you back to Dr. Nick."

Abby stared at the names and desperately wished she could erase them from the paper and from her life as well. "Who's this…this Joyce Beverly?"

"She was the gal in charge of the Montgomery Agency, that adoption agency from which your parents adopted you. She was a smart one, from what I learned later. She and that Wesby guy disappeared at the same time, just before the police raided the agency after the warehouse fire," the detective responded thoughtfully. "But I heard from some of the fellows on the force that Wesby and Beverly left the country before the FBI could question them."

The detective dug through numerous pieces of paper. "This is a big file, but it only has a few names of possible survivors."

Abby was carefully scrutinizing each page, and when he turned up another yellowed piece of paper, Abby quickly reached for it. "Can I see that page?" Abby asked nervously as she spotted Ruby's name at the bottom. "Is anyone from Ruby's family alive that you know of?"

At the bottom of the paper was a question mark along with the words: Ruby Cramden's father. Name: Arthur Cramden. Frequents homeless shelters. Last known address: Bixby Homeless Shelter, Richardson, New York.

"This Arthur Cramden. Do you suppose he's still alive?"

"I don't know, Abby. It's possible. From the reports I received later, Arthur Cramden would have been about fifty years old at that time…he could still be alive in his seventies…depends on what kind of a life he led and what shape his health was in."

Two other names were handwritten in the margin: one was the name of Dr. Luis Minolo, and the other name was Donna Ranno. "Who are these two, Uncle Don?"

"Dr. Minolo is the doctor who was in charge of the laboratory in Zenova where the big announcement was planned to be held. He was working with Dr. Nick. Donna Ranno was the supervising nurse in the warehouse when you and your family were imprisoned there. Sarah told me this Donna could have been a much bigger threat to her and to your family, except after you and your mother left with the group for Nortovia, this Donna came down with a serious flu and was out of commission for awhile. That left Sarah better able to help your Dad and the boys escape."

"I can barely make out this address under her name. Can you decipher it?"

"Let's see," said Don hoping he could read his own writing after all these years. "It seems to be 2040 S. Bingham or Brightham…maybe Bentham. The city looks like Rutheford, New York. I think that's quite a ways up state."

Abby carefully put the notes in her purse. "Thank you, Uncle Don. This list of names will help me figure out where to start on my search. This has been the most awful time of my life but I just knew you would help me gain some perspective."

Wiping away a tear, he held out his arms to her. "Be careful, Abby. This won't be easy."

She choked back the tears as she walked over to embrace the man who would always be her much loved uncle. He had given her a lot to think about and several avenues to pursue. But, had she realized the emotional struggles she would have to endure, she might have had second thoughts about leaving Vesta.

Chapter Ten

As Abigail slowly and sadly drove out of the city leaving her once normal life behind, the horror of the news she had received followed her like a shadow that clutched at her heart. And the information she had gotten from her uncle Don bounced back and forth through her mind, never settling…never falling into place. Somehow she would have to get a plan formulated to begin the search for her identity. She headed east toward New York and toward events she could hardly imagine.

At lunchtime she pulled into a diner outside the small town of Sanders. The diner was complete with neon signs dazzling the front, and once inside Abby was sure she had stepped back into time. The diner had the old fashioned malt machine, counter with swiveling red stools and low leather booths.

After ordering coffee and a small soup, she picked up her cell phone and called her supervisor and friend, Elaine. Abigail hoped she could make Elaine understand her abrupt departure from the hospital and the leave she would have to take from work. She had to convince her friend of the desperate situation she was facing, and yet withhold details. It would test their friendship and working relationship, but Elaine had been her advocate and support since they had met, and Abigail was counting on that.

"Elaine, this is Abby." A silence followed and then came the curt words to which she could only reply, "I know…I know…please take a minute to hear me out. I've encountered a horrendous problem and I'm the only one who can hope to take care of it. Would you….." The impatience in Elaine's voice was something Abby had not heard before and it saddened her. Elaine had supported her since their first meeting, but this hardly sounded like her friend.

"Abigail, it appears you've taken advantage of our friendship and of my support. Why did you just walk out of the hospital without notifying anyone, and especially without a doctor's release? And, what do you plan to do about your job?"

"I'm terribly sorry," Abby replied guiltily, "All I can ask is that you consider my past record and allow me time to get this terrible problem straightened out."

"The Board isn't going to like this, Abby." Then after a long pause Elaine continued, "You are one of our best nurses and my friend, so I'll try to give you some leeway here. You know we have to be able to depend on our nurses. I'll expect to hear something from you, say within two weeks. We'll list your absence as a vacation, but please remember Abby, two weeks tops. It's all the time I can give you before I'll have to make a determination regarding your future status with the hospital. We have rules to follow, you know."

As an afterthought Elaine commented, "Oh and please try to stop at a clinic somewhere and have a doctor look at you just to make sure you're all right. Then have him send the report to me. That'll help when Dr. Carlson sends in his evaluation with his comments."

"Thank you, Elaine. I know this isn't easy for you as my supervisor and I do appreciate it. I'll be in touch and...please pray for me." With that Abby closed her cell phone and tried to eat her soup without thinking about the problems that were pursuing her. She tried several spoonfuls and then pushed the bowl away, her appetite gone.

She decided to head toward the city of Richardson, New York, to pursue her search, wondering about the difficulties she might encounter. Her fears and doubts plagued her and she shuddered again thinking of her existence as a...***clone...***

"Oh Lord," she yelled into the silence of her car, "What *am* I? What is going to happen to me?" Then her voice trailed off in despair, "Am I still your child?" That question was one she would wonder about often.

She reached to turn off the music on the radio with a shaking hand. *I've got to get my mind on my task at hand or I'll go mad thinking about this...cloning. Richardson, that's the city...Richardson. How will I handle this? I guess the first thing would be to check with that Bixby Shelter.*

Her thoughts jumped to what might be ahead, and she wondered if she would ever find this man who was thought to be Ruby's father. And even if she found him, how would she feel about him? What would she even say to him? Her thoughts wandered...*Ruby. I wish I could at least have known you...*and a tear slowly ran down her cheek spilling onto her jacket.

Her thoughts drifted to her conversation with Elaine and her job at the hospital which was so important to her. Thoughts of losing that job and alienating those she had come to call her friends convinced her to do as Elaine had instructed.

Focusing on that task, as one task at a time was all she was capable of handling, she stopped at the first clinic she found in the next town on her way to Richardson. She was able to get a brief physical done by a doctor's assistant and the satisfactory results were quickly faxed to Vesta Memorial Hospital.

Well, that's done...now to continue to Richardson.

The remaining miles droned on and afternoon began ebbing into evening as she arrived in the city. Pulling into a filling station, she inquired about homeless shelters. The attendant looked at her quizzically as if she might not know what she was asking.

"The only one I know of, Lady, is the Bixby Shelter. It's about a mile up the road on this same street. Left side...you can't miss it."

Still wondering why a nice lady like her would want in a homeless shelter, he filled her gas tank, and then stood shaking his head as he watched her drive away.

The outskirts of Richardson were picturesque with lush green lawns and neatly kept homes, but the pleasant scenes soon morphed into an entirely different environment. The neon lights were beginning to flicker, giving downtown Richardson a seedy, run-down appearance. Glancing up ahead she made out the purple neon sign that displayed the words, "Bixby Homeless Shelter."

She apprehensively parked her car in the adjoining parking area, but now that she was finally here, she hesitated to go into the building. What would it be like? She had never been in a shelter for the homeless before.

Bracing herself, she locked the car and approached the front door. Several men stood to the side of the door and were eyeing her closely. She smiled slightly moving quickly for the door, but as she opened it, she wasn't prepared for what she saw. A television was blaring somewhere in the room, men of all ages and different plights were sprawled out in some form or other on the various couches and chairs. The stale air was almost enough to make her turn back and run to her car. But, she was determined.

Approaching what appeared to be the office, she tapped on the window. A woman at a desk wearily got up from her chair and opened the window through which they could speak. "Yes, what can I do for you?"

Abby tried to smile. "I'm looking for someone, a distant relative, and I thought you might be able to tell me if he's here, or if you know of him."

The woman sighed. It was the question they heard most often, and now she was going to have to try to find another lost relative. "Come on in. We'll talk where it's quieter," she said unlocking the side door to the office, and immediately locking it again once Abby had entered.

Chapter Eleven

As Abby waited in the shelter office with her many unanswered questions, Josh and Stephen sat in the back of the Vesta Community Christian Church trying to answer questions of their own.

"Abby's obviously still very upset. Why would she just leave without telling us, and just where was she going?" Stephen was edgy and got up to pace in the aisle of the church. "What a crazy thing to do," he continued. "Do you think she was in her right mind, Josh?"

Josh had been praying quietly and looked up quickly hearing the word "crazy". "Of course she isn't crazy, Stephen. I think she probably needed to find some answers about her identity." Yet as he spoke, doubts crept into his mind. "But, you know, I wonder what will happen and what she'll find. We don't even know where to look for her…and even if we did, would it be right for us to go after her or is it best that we let her handle it herself?"

Stephen responded sarcastically, "You sound like you're pretty unsure yourself, Josh. Isn't God answering your prayers?" Then, seeing the hurt in his brother's eyes, he softened. "Josh, I'm sorry. I'm frustrated and I'm taking it out on you."

Josh ignored his brother's apology as a thought suddenly occurred to him. "Stephen, who would you say would be the most likely person Abby would go to for help?"

Stephen frowned as if he had no clue, and then quickly came to the same thought his brother had. "I bet she'd go see Uncle Don. What'd you think?"

"I think so. Why don't we take a ride out to his place and see if he's seen her or talked to her?"

As he spoke, the small church choir filed in quietly and began to practice melodic familiar hymns. Stephen and Josh both turned toward the choir, listening intently. Within minutes their melancholy moods seemed to lift.

As the brothers left the church to find any information they could about their missing sister, the music of the choir followed them.

"I believe the Arthur Cramden you're looking for is the same man who comes here often, but he goes missing a lot. We never know where he is or what he's doing. Usually at night he shows up, but is gone right after breakfast."

Abby was getting hopeful and leaned over the old scratched desk to look at the papers the woman was checking. "Could you describe him for me please?"

The woman, who had finally introduced herself as Betty, looked up somewhat startled. "You don't know what he looks like? If he's a relative of yours, I would assume you'd know that." As Abby shook her head, Betty checked over the papers in her hand searching for some description of Arthur Cramden.

"The only thing I can tell you is that the man I'm thinking of as Arthur Cramden is quite thin and unkempt. Does that help?"

Abby smiled, thankful for any news she could get. "Is there any way you might find out if he's here now?"

"Well, I guess I could holler out there and see if anyone's seen him." Betty pulled her large frame out of the chair and walked into the massive living room which was more like the lobby of a bus terminal, and called out in a loud voice, "Anyone here know where Arthur Cramden is?"

Several heads turned in her direction and a few of the living corpses struggled to a semi-upward position. One man yelled a response before collapsing once again on his couch, "Ain't seen him since breakfast this morning."

Abby took a long look at the men and tears formed in her eyes. *These lost souls. Surely many of them must have a hope of doing something better in life, yet without proper help and training, they probably have no idea where to begin. Still, they too are God's children.*

Betty's voice broke into her thoughts, "You know, I'm thinking maybe it would be a good idea for you to come early tomorrow and help serve breakfast. The fellow I think is your Arthur Cramden is usually around for breakfast so you might have a pretty good chance to see him and...we could sure use the help."

Abby was grateful for the suggestion and grateful to leave the sadness of her surroundings. She consented to be there at 6:00 in the morning and handed Betty her business card asking her to call if Arthur Cramden did show up that evening.

Before leaving the shelter, she walked gingerly to the couch of the man who seemed to have some knowledge of Arthur Cramden. He didn't appear to be conscious as she approached, but as she tapped him firmly on the shoulder, she got a rise out of him.

"Hey lady, what'd ya want? I'm sleepin' here."

Abby took a five dollar bill out of her purse and held it so the man could see it. "I need to know what Arthur Cramden looks like. You seem to know who he is."

Seeing the money, the man became more cooperative and more awake. "Well, there's lots 'a guys here, but I'm pretty shur he's a small guy...about seventy maybe, and real thin." He seemed satisfied with his own answer and grabbed for the money. "Oh, and he don't like to shave...grey hair all over, head and face."

Abby was glad to give him the money for the help and quickly left the building to find a clean fresh motel room and get mentally prepared for the next morning.

Detective Donovan didn't seem at all surprised to see Josh and Stephen at his door. "Come on in. I'm really glad to see you two...been awhile."

Stephen couldn't wait for the niceties and hastily questioned, "Have you seen Abby? Did she come here?"

Josh reached over to touch Stephan's arm in a gesture to calm him down, but Stephen was adamant. "She had some terrible news and collapsed, so Josh took her to the hospital. But, then she left without telling anyone. When we talked to Sarah all she said was that Abby was determined to find some answers."

Josh interrupted to make amends for his brother's impatience. "We're very upset, Uncle Don, as I'm sure you can imagine. We just don't know where she is and if she's even well enough mentally and physically to have left the hospital. Please tell us anything you might know."

The Detective knew this would be a difficult discussion. He extended his arm and ushered them into the living room. He had to be honest with these young men, they were his family.

"Please sit down...want anything to drink?" Stephen and Josh shook their heads and as Stephen looked like he was about to question him further, the detective sat down next to them. "I think you know Abby was here. I guess I've always been one of the first people she's gone to whenever she's had problems...and this one is the biggest problem she's faced. You know about it, of course?"

"Yes, we know and we're terribly upset to know what she's going through," Josh responded. "What did you tell her?"

The detective's aging eyes couldn't hide the pain he felt for his dear Abby. "I showed her all the information I have in the file, and gave her names of those people who might possibly still be alive. She seemed to have an urgent need to find anyone who might be able to help her find some identity. She seems to be trying to find out just who she is and, according to her, *what* she is. She's hoping desperately that whoever she finds alive will be able to shed some light on those things."

"Can you tell us the names of those people she might be trying to locate?" Stephen asked, more calm now as the discussion was progressing.

"I have it in the file. Just a minute and I'll get it." Detective Donovan found the file and brought it out for the second time that day. "There's a lot of information in it, but you can look at it."

"I honestly don't know what to do," Josh answered, almost hopelessly. "Would it make sense for us to take off and try to find her, or is this something she has to do by herself?"

"No!" Stephen interjected. "She shouldn't be out there by herself. We need to be with her."

At that point the detective knew he needed to comment. He had been avoiding offering an opinion, but now it was time. "I hope you'll understand my position in this discussion, fellas, but I feel strongly that this is something Abby has to handle by herself. When she was here she seemed physically sound and after our talk, I felt her emotional state was much better than when she arrived."

"Are you sure of that?" Stephen queried. "I won't be able to rest unless I'm sure her doing this by herself is the best thing. She is a young woman and so much can happen to her."

Josh countered, "Stephen, I'll admit she's young and she could be vulnerable, but I know for a fact her faith in the Lord is strong and I firmly believe that he will be with her every minute."

"OK, OK," Stephen gave in. "If you two are so convinced, I'll defer to you. But Uncle Don, if she contacts you would you let us know how she is and how she's doing in her search? Be sure to tell her we love her and we're praying for her."

Josh was pleased to hear his brother actually speak of praying but didn't let on that it made an impact on him. "Well, thanks for the list, Uncle Don. Now we'll have a guide to her possible whereabouts while she's gone. Next time we see you we hope it will be under less stressful conditions."

As the young men left the apartment, the detective stood and watched them until they disappeared down the staircase. *Good guys,* he thought as he closed the door, but instead of putting the papers back in the overstuffed file, he sat down to read them all over again.

Chapter Twelve

I wonder what life stories I'd hear from these men who have obviously had some bad breaks, Abby thought as she walked through the lobby of the shelter at 6:00 in the morning. She followed the instructions to the area that appeared to be the kitchen in the north wing. The smells emanating from that area were good hearty smells and fortunately replaced the smells of the lobby area.

Opening the squeaking double doors to the kitchen, she was amazed to see at least five or six cooks working feverishly over what appeared to be eggs, bacon and waffles. The aroma of fresh coffee renewed her and she nodded toward the coffee urns to one of the cooks and was given the high sign to help herself.

"I'm Abby and I told Betty I'd help dish up the breakfast for the men this morning."

"Help?" chuckled one of the cooks. "You're probably it. Don't get too many volunteers here at this time of day."

Abby found an apron hanging on a nail near the door and draped it around herself, then walked to one of the ovens to see what she could do to help.

By 6:30 she was positioned behind the three warming tables in the dining room and prayed for the ability to handle the job before her. The cook was right. She was it…the only volunteer with three large ladles, three entrees and who knew how many men to feed.

The door to the dining room opened with a bang and several men almost ran up to get their food. As Abby did her best to dish everything up quickly, the line was forming fast by men with empty stomachs. She smiled and tried to speak to them as they went through the line. Many were excited to get their food. It was probably their only meal until dinner at the shelter. Other men stumbled up to the food trays and could barely function, hands and bodies shaking. This was something Abby had never experienced and as she looked at the many desperate men, her heart melted and filled with compassion. *Maybe Arthur Cramden is one of these desperate people who needed compassion as well. No matter what his past, this is truly no life.*

She tried to look each man over carefully, hoping desperately that she would find someone matching the description she had of Arthur Cramden. Then during the busiest time, she unknowingly dished up his food while turning to get another spoon from one of the cooks and in so doing, missed him.

Arthur Cramden, Ruby Cramden's infamous father, couldn't take his eyes off the woman dishing up his food. He almost lost control as he stumbled up to the line and looked at her. *It's Ruby! Ruby! My beautiful Ruby!* Now as he was close he was able to get a good look at her. *She looks just like Ruby...but it couldn't be her. She's so young and Ruby would be, what... 'bout fifty now? How kin this be? Nobody could look that much like someone else...it ain't possible.* As he continued through the line, his mind was so confused he almost forgot to find a table and he just stood there holding his plate. *Should I try to talk to her? Or mabe jist better to get out a here, and pretend I never seen her.*

As the breakfast line thinned, Abby was discouraged. She hadn't seen anyone who fit the description of Ruby's father...but then, she did have to look away several times. *Maybe I missed him. I'll just check out everybody when I'm done here.*

As soon as the men were fed, the large warming pans were lifted onto the carts, and she was excused. She looked from one end of the dining room to the other searching for anyone resembling Arthur Cramden. As she studied the men at the tables, one man got up, put his dishes in the dish tray and almost ran from the room. *Could that be him?* Abby wondered excitedly as she stood on tip toes to get a better look at the man hurriedly limping out of the dining area. It did resemble the description she had gotten of him. The man was slight of build with grey hair and beard and tattered clothes.

Abby ran to the kitchen to hang up her apron and left quickly through the squeaking doors. As she reached the lobby she caught a glimpse of a grey-haired man leaving the building. She had a hard time getting to the door because several of the men stood in front of her thanking her for helping make their breakfast special. Although Abby wasn't sure just what the intent was, she accepted it graciously. By the time she reached the sidewalk the grey-haired man was out of sight.

As she stood helplessly looking down the street, a young man leaning against the building busily smoking a cigar asked if he could help her.

"I'd sure appreciate it if you could. I was trying to catch up with a man who just left the shelter. He had a grey beard...grey hair...small man about seventy years old?"

"Yah. I seen him. He was doin' pretty good to run with a limp like he's got. He's one of them guys that sometimes hangs out under the 10th Street Bridge. They go there and find whatever they kin to get 'em a few bucks."

Abby was grateful for the information but before she could get to her car and go after the old man, the young smoker grabbed her arm. "Hey, that news ain't fur free. Got a five spot?" She apprehensively opened her purse but found only four dollars in small bills. The man grabbed the money. After all, four bucks is four bucks. As she headed for her car parked on the side of the building, she realized she didn't even know where the 10th Street Bridge was. "Hey!" she yelled once more for help from the man by the door, "where is the bridge from here?"

He motioned to his right, and she left quickly.

Stephen resigned himself to head back home to New York after he and Josh left the detective's apartment. The thought of how he'd be welcomed nagged at him because of Tiffany's responses on the phone. He had never been sure what had changed her from the young woman who seemed to love him to the indifferent person she had become.

Maybe I did something, or most likely I just worked too hard and neglected her and the twins. Still I wonder if that would have been enough to change her so. "Whatever the problem is," he said to himself as he headed his car toward the Big Apple, "I'll just have to try harder."

Josh had given his brother a pamphlet to read about God's views on marriage with accompanying verses in the Bible as a reference, but Stephen only took the material to avoid the inevitable discussion.

Stephen was well on his way back to New York by the time Josh delved into the subject of his upcoming sermon which he entitled, "How are we to respond to people others think of as society's outcasts?"

Chapter Thirteen

The Tenth Street Bridge was in the same area as the shelter, which caused a tinge of fear for Abby as she eased her car into a parking space along the street facing the bridge. This was not a neighborhood affording safety to a young attractive woman. She locked the car securely as she tucked her long red hair under her jacket with the collar up and put on dark glasses. There was no defined path into the area under the bridge so she decided to take a walk on the bridge and look down at the area below from that vantage point.

It took her a few minutes to reach the arch of the bridge so she could scan the underbelly with all its garbage, papers and junk strewn in every direction as if a naughty child had a tantrum there. *Wow, do I really want to go down there?* Abby thought as she spotted several ragged people hunched up against the walls and a number of teens who were hanging around as if looking for trouble wherever they could find it.

She stood at her spot on the bridge letting the breeze blow around her as she tried to determine what to do. Looking down, she saw what looked like the man from the shelter kicking the scattered debris on the path, but it was difficult to be sure from the bridge. The man seemed to match the description she had gotten of Arthur Cramden, as incomplete as that was, and he also resembled the brief look she had of the man leaving the shelter. So, in spite of her trepidation, she decided to enter the world of the unknowns under the bridge.

Stephen pulled into his driveway as the afternoon sun was beginning its decent, and was delighted when the twins left their ballgame in the front yard to run to greet him. The boys were one of the few joys in his melancholy life, and even at eight years of age were showing great athletic promise. Jason was the larger of the two and was already handsome for his age. He was like his father and was inquisitive about world events, displaying an energetic fascination with geography.

Jeremy, although slighter in build, was the more athletic of the two. He was competitive, yet respectful, in his association with team mates and his twin. Both boys had shocks of red/brown hair, which Stephen attributed to his wife whose hair was one of her most striking attributes.

"Dad, throw some balls to us. We need all the practice we can get. The big game is Thursday and we gotta be ready."

"Yah, and make them real fast balls, Dad. Those are the kind we'll have to learn so we can turn around and pick off a guy on base."

The next hour was the highlight of the day for Stephen as he threw one fast ball after another to his eager basemen. It was a welcome brief escape from his worry about his sister and his marriage.

When he finally managed to break away from his big league hopefuls, he opened the kitchen door and hoped desperately that he might get some enthusiastic response there. But the kitchen was empty with no sign of dinner.

"Hi Tiff, I'm home. How about going out to eat with the boys," he called as he glanced around the kitchen once again. "Tiff? Tiff?"

He trudged upstairs to the bedroom area and was surprised to see his wife perched on the edge of the bed. Her silk blue eyes were swollen and red, and as she saw him coming she tried to turn away so he couldn't see her face. "Oh, I didn't know you'd be home so early. That's why there's no dinner fixed, and no, I don't want to go out and eat."

In spite of the cold atmosphere Tiffany had created, Stephen felt a love and passion for his wife, and was almost brought to tears himself to see how their relationship had disintegrated. He slowly approached her and touched her shoulder gently.

"Tiff, what is it? Why have you been crying? Did I do something? Please tell me," he pleaded in desperation, "and I'll do whatever I can to make it right."

For a brief moment she seemed to relax under his touch once again, but just as quickly she bristled. "What makes you think anything with this marriage can be made right? It took years to get it this way, and if it were ever to work again I suppose it would take years for that too."

Stephen, in his deep sadness, reached for her and pulled her up to him to embrace her.

"Stephen, it's not that simple. The fact is, I don't know if I love you anymore."

The words cut into his very soul and he had to sit on the bed to steady himself. *How could this have happened? We loved each other so.*

"Tiffany, you can't mean that. We loved each other so passionately for years, how can you say you don't know if you love me?"

As Tiffany slumped into a chair she could only shake her head back and forth in despair. She began crying and soon the cries developed into sobs. Stephen could do nothing. He tried to talk to her, to hug her, to smooth her hair, but nothing helped. It was as if she had already left him and he was totally alone in their room.

He jammed his hand into his pocket and in so doing dislodged the pamphlet that Josh had given him on making marriage work. Tiffany watched the paper fall to the floor and read the heading. "Where'd you get that," she whispered, and reached for it. "Did your brother give you this?"

Stephen knew that was the end of discussion about the booklet. Tiffany had developed resentment for Josh in the last year that he couldn't explain. Josh hadn't done or said anything that would have made her upset, yet she held to this anger towards him.

Without a word, he took the pamphlet from her and set it on his dresser. "Maybe reading it wouldn't help anyway."

"Oh, Stephen. I don't think I can love you as I used to, so many things have happened that have changed all that."

"Well, what can we do about it?" Stephen asked intently. "Should we go for counseling? I'm willing to do whatever I can to help you love me again. After all, we have two wonderful boys to think about too."

The next hour and a half was an exercise of futility. Tiffany was unable to describe her feelings and Stephen was unable to accept the finality in her voice.

"Please Hon, let me call Matthew Peterson. He's one of the best marriage counselors at the church. Even though we don't attend often, I'm sure he'd be willing to see us. Would you at least come with me and talk over things with him? Please, please?"

Tiffany looked at her husband. She had never seen him like this. He was unraveling before her very eyes. "Alright, I'll try it, but if it doesn't help, I'm out of there."

Stephen knew that would be all the discussion for the evening, but if they would go to counseling, there was a chance at working things out. That ray of hope for his marriage, however, didn't extend to the nightmare his sister was going through and the horrendous news they had all received.

Josh sat at his desk for some time after his brother left. He began by outlining his sermon for Sunday, and then found himself staring into space reflecting on the disturbing events happening in his family. His heart was breaking for his sister, and now his brother was in an unhappy marriage situation with a dwindling faith that could have sustained him…and he seemed to be unable to help either of them.

His thoughts ended abruptly when the phone rang. He wasn't sure he was ready to take any calls now, especially if someone needed help. He needed time to pray and regain his sense of ability first.

Hesitantly he answered, "Pastor Josh here."

"Pastor. This is Cindy, the nurse from the hospital who was with your sister. I hope you don't mind my calling, but I am so concerned about her. I know she left the hospital unexpectedly and I have no idea how she is. Would you be able to share any news with me?"

Josh had to admit that even though he had family problems to face, he was quite pleased to hear from her. He couldn't help but be impressed with her concern for Abby, and he suspected her interest in the family might include him as well.

"Nice of you to call, Cindy. You were a caring and helpful nurse to my sister and I appreciate your concern for her. Abby left the hospital to try to handle a problem that had come up for her, and I guess she felt leaving was the right decision. To my knowledge, she is all right."

The conversation casually drifted into other topics until Josh surprised himself by asking her if she'd like to meet him for coffee at a nearby coffee shop. She readily accepted and they arranged to meet in an hour. That would hopefully give Josh enough time to do more work on his sermon.

Later as he grabbed his jacket and made sure he had his wallet, he found himself strangely excited to see her again. The anticipation of the get-together seemed to push his family problems somewhat into the background, and he whistled a happy tune as he headed for the coffee shop.

Chapter Fourteen

The teenage boys pointed at her, rolled their eyes and snickered as she approached their den under the 10th Street Bridge. Normally she wouldn't have been concerned to meet several teenagers, but these boys were different. They were sharing a bottle of whiskey and laughing heartily. She quickly changed course and headed for the river side of the bridge hoping to find the man she so wanted to talk to.

Fortunately the boys didn't pursue her and she breathed a "thank-you." It seemed to Abby that her life the last few days had been a series of prayers, one after another, and she had to hang on to the hope that God would still hear her prayers, no matter what.

She had trouble walking through papers, bottles and debris of all kinds that were housed under the bridge. Minutes passed as she continued her search and she was getting discouraged. She was about to turn around and leave when out of the corner of her eye she saw a figure duck behind one of the bridge pillars. As she slowly approached the area she could see it was the man from the shelter...the one she thought might be Arthur. He saw her and turned to run, but he caught his foot on a stone and fell noiselessly to the ground.

"Oh, let me help you," Abby called out and hurried to his side. The man looked up at her and then quickly looked away, afraid of what he might discover. Abby took his arm and lifted him up to a standing position. It was then she saw the pain in his eyes.

She didn't want to waste any more time so she boldly asked, "Are you Arthur Cramden?" The look in his eyes was that of a deer caught in the headlights of an oncoming car.

"Why ya want him?" was his response as he looked around for a quick way to escape this woman who obviously wanted to talk to him.

"I need to know some things and Arthur Cramden is a man who might help me. Are you that man?" Abby was trying hard to be patient, but after all this time she wanted to get any information she could.

"OK, so I'm the guy…what'd ya want me for?"

Abby was encouraged. "Mr. Cramden, could we talk a few minutes? We could maybe go to a café and I'd be happy to buy you some food while we talk."

The food part sounded good to Arthur, but the talking…well, that could be something else. "Yah, OK, but don't know what ya'd want ta talk ta me about."

It took half an hour to walk Arthur Cramden out of the underbelly of the bridge. For a man who was able to limp so quickly out of the shelter that morning, Abby was surprised he moved so slowly and with obvious pain. Within a short two blocks after leaving the bridge, Arthur pointed out a café and they walked to it, making an odd looking pair.

As Abby walked with the gaunt looking man who could very well be Ruby's father, she hoped for any information from him that would help put some puzzle pieces of her life in place.

Miles away in Vesta, David approached Sarah's apartment at the Vesta Senior Nursing Facility and hoped desperately that she would help him find his Abby. When Sarah opened the door she was surprised and most pleased to see David…but in the back of her mind she knew why he was there.

"Come in, David. How nice to see you."

"Sarah, I'll only stay a minute, but I really need a few answers, and I'm hoping you can help me."

Motioning for David to sit, Sarah pulled her shawl tightly around her as if it was a protective shield. "How can I help you, David?"

"Please know that I love Abby with all my heart…more than any girl I've ever known, but I'm desperate to know where she is and how she is."

Sarah sat slowly on her overstuffed couch and secretly hoped she'd sink down so far she wouldn't have to answer him. But, as she looked into his eyes she couldn't mistake the love he had for Abby. "My dear young man, I would love to tell you where she is, but I truly don't know. All I can share with you is that she learned some devastating news and has gone to find some answers. I'm sorry I can't tell you more than that. I hope you understand."

David knew from the sadness in Sarah's eyes that she was telling him all she was able to. "Is there anyone else I might talk to for some answers, Sarah?"

The elderly woman, whose great love for Abby may not even be as strong as David's love for her, slowly walked to her desk and wrote down Detective Donovan's address. "I think you might find the detective to be of more help than I can be, but David, please pursue this according to God's will or it may turn out tragically for both you and Abby."

David smiled and instinctively gave Sarah a hearty hug as he thanked her profusely and left to see Detective Donovan.

As Abby approached the cafe with the old man she felt physically ill. Her thoughts never stopped bombarding her as the word *clone* echoed through her very being. She looked over at her companion and wondered wearily why it made any difference at all if he was Ruby's father. Her life was so full of upheaval over the news of her cloning that she had to concentrate fully on her present whereabouts or lose the reality of it.

Arthur glanced at her often out of the corner of his eye. *So unhappy. Even her smile don't hide it.*

When they reached the café, Abby mechanically opened the door and took the first booth. Arthur was somewhat surprised because the booth was full of food scraps and the table still held the last customer's dirty dishes. Abby didn't seem to notice at first until Arthur spoke. "OK lady, so we're here. Now what'ja want from me?"

"What? What did you say?" Abby responded, forcing herself into the moment. Here she was, sitting across from the man who was most likely Ruby's father. She had to concentrate…she had to be strong…stop the self-pity.

"Here's the thing, Arthur. For personal reasons I have to find several people to fit some pieces of my life together, and you're one of those people."

Arthur looked at her as though she was out of her mind. "And ya think I can put somethin' together for ya? What would a guy like me have that ya'd want anyhow?"

"I'll get right to the point …" Abby began until she acknowledged the waitress standing impatiently at their booth. Abby gave her order for coffee and toast, remembering to eat something even though she wasn't hungry.

"Arthur, what'll you have? I'm buying."

Those last two words perked Arthur up. He hadn't eaten much breakfast at the shelter after his shock of seeing the woman who looked so much like his Ruby. So with this opportunity he had been given, he rattled off an amount of food that would have pleased a sumo wrestler. Satisfied that he'd have a good meal, he glanced up at Abby. "Ya, well…go on."

"The point is," Abby began again, "I need to know if you are related to a Ruby Cramden, and if so, I'd like to hear everything you can tell me about her and your relationship with her. Don't you think the meal is worth enough to give me a little time?"

The man's body language told Abby that once again he felt uncomfortable and would have a difficult time talking.

"Ya, I'm Arthur Cramden, Ruby's father. So what!"

Abby was surprised at the tears that formed in her eyes. This man, this derelict, this angry, unhappy man was Ruby's father, so was he…her grandfather? As the reality of that thought hit her, she stuttered, "Please, please tell me all you know. What was she like? Was she nice? Did you love her?"

His first response was rather hostile. "I ain't seen her in years." But, as he looked at the sadness in the young woman's face, he began to speak more carefully. "Ruby was one in a million. She was a real beaut'… you look a lot like her...same red hair, same eyes. When I seen you at the shelter I thought for a minute Ruby come back."

Abby observed him carefully for any bit of emotion, but seeing none she continued to listen intently. "She was a feisty one, that Ruby. 'Course I didn't help much. I boozed it up pretty good there for awhile, and the ladies liked me then. My ol' lady never did understan' that. So, one day I just up and left the two of them. Never seen 'em again. I guess the ol' lady died, and I heard Ruby went to jail for awhile…but then Ruby wouldn't have nothin' to do with me even if I seen her."

"Did you ever hear anything about Ruby after you heard she was in jail?" Abby pressed on.

The old man gazed at her. "Man, you sure do look like her. If I din't know better, I'd sure as heck think you was her. Are you related or somethin'?"

"I might be, Mr. Cramden, but I need to find out everything I can about her. I heard she died over in the country of Nortovia, so I missed knowing her and now I can only rely on what other people tell me about her."

"Well, you kin see I don't know much ta help ya lady."

By the time his food arrived he dove into it like it was a treasure he'd been searching for. While he ate voraciously, Abby sipped on the strong coffee and tried to down the dry toast.

Subconsciously she talked as if to herself, "Why did God take her away before I even knew her?"

"What?" the man asked, looking up from the mound of food before him.

"Oh…I was just asking God a question. He's always taken care of me, but now I'm in a situation I don't understand and Ruby, the one person who could help me, can't. I just wondered why God would work that way."

Now Abby had his undivided attention. He put his fork down and stared at her. "You mean you believe in that stuff? Never made sense to me. Who needs it anyway?"

Abby was suddenly alert. "*You* need him, Mr. Cramden. Your life might have been so different if you had believed in God. He has a way of touching lives that brings peace to the mind, strength to the body and love to the heart."

"Ya, right!" the old man retorted.

Abby was undeterred as she remembered a story her father told her many times and how it helped him come to a faith in God. "I have a question, Arthur. Say you fell off a ship into the ocean and were drowning because you couldn't swim to save yourself. Then someone threw you a life preserver. What would you do?"

"Stupid question. I'd grab it, 'a course. What's that got to do with anythin'?"

"Look at it this way," Abby continued. "Think of all the years you used alcohol and women to satisfy you. Did it ever work?" He reluctantly shook his head. "Well, there you are. You can't swim…get it? Thing is, God's been throwing you a life preserver all your life but you haven't taken hold of it. You just ignore him. So, when you die, you'll drown, so to speak."

"Drown?" the old man choked, grabbing a glass of water. "What'da mean, drown?"

"Well, God's planned a heaven for you, but you seem to prefer to drown in your own mess of sins. If you had come to God early in your life and relied on him to help you, you could have had an entirely different life: a better one, a good one." Abby took another sip of the coffee before going on.

"Not only that, Arthur. God's Son, Jesus Christ, died on a cross two thousand years ago to pay the price for every sin you ever did, *and* to give you a very special gift."

Arthur was getting interested. "Ya, what gift?"

"Let me start out by asking you what you think will happen to you when you die."

Arthur snorted with laughter. "Well lady. I guess I'll be dead." Then looking at Abby curiously he added sarcastically, "Ya think that hell thing is for real that I hear about at the shelter meetins'?" He went back to consuming his food expecting her to tell him she didn't believe in that hell thing.

Instead, Abby said emphatically, "Yes I do! And from all I've read, hell is the very last place I would want to go to when I die. The gift Jesus offers us is the gift of heaven. If you've heard about that hell thing at the shelter, you probably also heard about how wonderful heaven is."

As he nodded somewhat cautiously, she added, "That's the greatest gift of all. Do you know in heaven you'd be happy and healthy? You'd never have to worry about a place to sleep or what to eat...and, no more pain. It's a miraculous place."

"Ya, well then, how'd ya get there instead of hell?"

Abby could see that this man, the man she now knew was part of her heritage, a grandfather of sorts, was becoming interested in what she was saying.

"There's a verse in the Bible that tells us for sure that we've *all* sinned and don't live up to God's plan, yet God declares us all 'not guilty.' Not guilty, Arthur. That means all the things you've done that you hate, would disappear before God. See, when you trust in Jesus Christ, you would be one of those he died for. Does that help to answer your question?"

Arthur nodded slowly and after a lengthy pause opened up to Abby. "I didn't tell you everything about Ruby. She was a good kid. She always helped her mother at home and even did little jobs for people to earn money. She smiled lots, even had some friends. She could'a had a better life after her ma died if I'd a been there…but I didn't show up. I heard she was livin' out on the streets after that and doin' anythin' to make money. So ya see, I was a bad person…a sinner like you said. Still am."

The café was rapidly filling up with young tattooed men who eyed her in a way that made her uncomfortable and she wanted to get back to the safety of her motel. She was pleased to hear what the old man finally said about Ruby. It helped a lot.

"I need to be going, Arthur, but I'd like to see you again. Would that be OK with you?"

Without hesitation, he nodded. "Ya gotta go already? I kinda liked talkin' to ya…like bein' with Ruby again," and Abby's heart melted.

"Before I go I want you to take my card and this $100 bill. I also have a little book here I hope you'll read. It's a Bible. It'll help you to understand better what we've been talking about."

As Abby stood, she was compelled to lean over and kiss his cheek, full of furry whiskers and all. He looked up startled and smiled broadly.

"Arthur, I'm so glad I found you. Will you be in this area when I return sometime soon?"

He looked up and Abby could see sadness in his eyes. "Ya, I'll be here. Thanks. I might even read the book. So long, lady," and then glancing at her card he shyly said, "Abigail."

Abby hastily left the café before the tears started and before the tattooed ones decided to follow her. She headed for her car thinking of Arthur Cramden. The day had been successful in several ways; she had learned more about Ruby, and spent time with Ruby's father. As she reached her car, she glanced back toward the little café and seemed to know in her heart that Mr. Arthur Cramden was going to be all right.

Chapter Fifteen

After introductions had been exchanged between David and Detective Donovan in the doorway of the detective's apartment, David was graciously ushered in. When the detective learned what Abby meant to the young man, he had a good idea of why he had come.

"This has been an exceptionally special day for me," the detective began. "I've had more company today than I have for some time. David, how can I help you?"

Before answering David blurted out, "So you're Uncle Don? It's great to finally meet you." Then, gaining his composure once again he took a chair opposite the detective and looked directly into his eyes. "I have to find Abby, and Sarah thought you might possibly know where I might start my search."

The detective squirmed inwardly as he struggled with his dilemma. *He seems like a nice young man, and he's obviously interested in Abby...but my first allegiance is to her and I can't betray her need to find identity, even if it means disappointing him.*

"You know, David, I'm caught between a rock and a hard place here. I can understand your desire to find Abby, but at the same time I feel I need to respect her privacy. If she didn't tell you herself what her plans were, she must not want you to know."

Detective Donovan grabbed for his pipe and lit the waiting tobacco to give himself time to contemplate the situation. "On one hand, David, if you could find her and join her, I'm sure everyone here would breathe easier knowing she was safe. On the other, she might be terribly upset if you found her. She has a grave problem and I just don't know which avenue would be best for either of you."

The detective got up from his chair motioning for David to join him in the kitchen. "Let's have some coffee and chat awhile before I decide how to handle this. You drink coffee, David?"

"Oh yes. Too much, I'm afraid. It bothers my sleep at times." He smiled at the detective and followed him into the neatly kept kitchen. Within a few minutes they were chatting amiably at the table over steaming cups of coffee and enticing éclairs. They liked each other at once and felt comfortable wherever the conversation led them. But, after an hour Detective Donovan could tell that David was getting antsy.

"David, I can't in all conscience help you find Abby without her permission. She trusts me and that's terribly important to me. But, I'll tell you what," the detective continued trying to be upbeat, "if I hear from Abby, and I feel strongly that I will, I'll tell her of your visit and your earnest desire to help her. Then she can decide for herself."

David's face fell and he set his coffee down as if making sure he didn't drop it. The detective was truly grieved to see how upset David was and tried to cheer him.

"David, I truly think that after Abby is out there awhile by herself, she'll have had time to think and to be alone, and she may very well want you to join her. Can we leave it at that for now?"

"Deal," agreed David as he stood to shake hands with the man he had come to respect in just a short time. "Thanks for being truthful with me and for justifying Abby's trust in you. I'll hang tight until I hear something."

As the detective walked David to the door, he patted him on the shoulder and wished him well. He was drawn to the sincerity of this young man who had quietly revealed his deep love for Abby.

The coffee house was bustling with customers taking their afternoon coffee breaks, while at a small table nestled in the back corner Josh and Cindy enjoyed each other's company. Josh blushed when he caught himself admiring her. At the hospital the situation was so chaotic that he hadn't taken a careful look at her, besides she was in her nurses' uniform. But today, she had on a dark pink pants suit with a top that made her look like a model. Her hair curled attractively, and her makeup flawless. He found her bubbly disposition to be uplifting and charming, and he had the feeling he could stay right there visiting with her the rest of the day.

Cindy was obviously interested in Josh and persisted in asking questions about his life, his work and his church. She hung on his every word, which he found pleasantly obvious. "I'm so glad that Abby is at least doing better," she reiterated from their earlier conversation. "I was so worried about her. Where do you think she is?" Then realizing she was getting too personal added, "Oh, I'm sorry. That really isn't my business, and I don't expect you to go further with that question. Just let her know if, or when, you talk to her that I have been very concerned and will be praying for her."

Ah, thought Josh when she mentioned praying. *I wonder if she's a Christian. Maybe I can even get her to our church.* "Cindy, do you go to church? That may be too personal a question too, so answer only if you'd like to."

"I do, yes. I'm a member of Our Savior's Church on Dover Street, but I'd love to come to your church sometime. You have a reputation for giving terrific sermons."

Josh was elated. "Come this Sunday. I'm preaching on how we should respond to people others think of as society's outcasts. I'm working on it tonight."

"I'll be there. Thanks for the invite," Cindy answered smiling, and the rest of the coffee time was spent in mutual admiration as they got to know each other better.

Stephen sat on the bed disconsolately as he listened to his wife crying in their adjoining bathroom. He was desperate. He loved her. She and the boys were his joy, but he had no idea what was wrong and no idea how to solve the situation even if he knew.

He reached for the phone and called Matthew Peterson to make an appointment for a marriage counseling session. He was able to get one for Friday of that week and was told by the secretary that the first session would be two hours. As he hung up the phone, he found himself praying for God's help in their marriage.

Tiffany, my dear Tiffany. If you just knew how much I love you, and how much unhappiness I have in our marriage too. And I can't even tell you of the horrific news about Abby that is causing such suffering in my family.

Sarah had been shaky since Abby told her of her plans to look for her identity. She didn't like the way she had been feeling since then. Her heart seemed to skip beats, she was short of breath at times, and she found herself resting more than usual. Eventually her concern for Abby prompted her call to Detective Donovan.

Her hand shook as she dialed his number, but his greeting was so cheerful that she immediately calmed. "Sarah, how good to hear from you. Are you doing all right, dear? I had planned to call you this afternoon and talk over Abby's situation."

"Don, I'm doing all right, I guess…little shaky and short of breath…but I'll be fine. I know Abby was going to stop and see you, so I took the liberty to call and see what frame of mind she was in when you talked with her."

"She did stop, Sarah, and we went through my file of investigations involving her, ah, situation. She seemed to be a little more rational and composed after we chatted awhile. She was eager to learn names of those people involved who might still be alive, and she was particularly interested in Ruby's father who was last known to live in a homeless shelter in New York. I have the feeling she was going to look for him first."

As Don shared with Sarah there was an undercurrent of concern for Sarah's health as well. "You sure you're all right?"

"Oh Don, I'm an old lady. Even if I wasn't all right, I'm happy to know that when I do die I'll just be making the awesome transition from one life to a vastly better one."

"Well Sarah, I think I can safely tell you that I personally feel Abby will find what she's looking for. She'll probably have to suffer during her search and some of the roads she takes may bring her heartache for a time, but I feel confident she will be OK."

"Thank you, Don. I do feel better now that I've talked to you. Please come and see me some time soon, and pray for our Abby, will you?"

Don sat quietly deep in thought after hanging up the phone. How privileged he was to be a part of this special family, and to be treated as a true uncle. He was filled with thankfulness, and although he was still learning about faith in God, he prayed for the special young woman he had loved as a niece all these years and prayed that she would have the ability to handle the difficulties she was bound to experience.

Chapter Sixteen

Only time and God would tell if the first road Abby had pursued would be a successful part of her life puzzle. Meeting Ruby's father had been somewhat fearful at first, but then so rewarding. Her heart ached for the unhappy little man who seemed to know nothing but selfishness and defeat throughout his life. He hadn't taken advantage of the opportunities he could have had as a husband and father...he had completely missed it, and in so doing had missed the chance to get to know his own daughter.

But maybe there's hope for some kind of a relationship for Arthur and me. I know I will see him again, and I can't help but feel somehow, some way, he'll be all right.

The tears rolling down her cheeks easily found the familiar path where so many tears had fallen before. Questions still plagued her and she cried out for help, "Please help me to know who I am."

As she drove aimlessly north out of Richardson, she began thinking about the nurse, Donna. *What kind of a woman was she? Sarah was sure Donna was part of Dr. Nick's secret scheme.* "I wonder how it would be to talk to her and watch her try to explain her part in those infamous plans." Abby mused out loud. "Maybe I'll just head up state to Rutheford and see if I can find her."

Driving through the Catskill Mountains was good therapy for Abby. The beauty enthralled her and for the moment she was able to shift that awful shadow to the back of her mind. She felt a strange peace as the mountains surrounded her. She had always loved the rich green forests and streams, so on an impulse she pulled her car into one of the scenic views to gaze in awe at the majesty before her. Truly God had done a magnificent job forming the earth to accommodate man and the numerous creatures.

The creatures God formed…the millions of people he created…making a home for us. She smiled thinking about the mighty hand of God, but quickly the ominous thoughts returned and spoiled her pleasant reflection.

God created millions of people, but did God create ME??

Just as quickly, the peace of the mountains left her and she became filled with apprehension and doubts as to what her investigations would actually reveal about her personhood. Shivering in the cool air, she quickly retreated to her car and continued her journey towards Rutheford in the foothills of the mountains. The route she had taken off the interstate was a country road with glistening shade trees bent over giving shelter and shade.

Up ahead she spotted a sign bent with age indicating that Rutheford was five miles ahead. An assortment of eating places was advertised on an adjacent sign, and Abby committed those to memory. Her stomach had been reminding her the last few miles that she hadn't eaten for awhile, and she determined that would be first on her agenda.

Rutheford seemed to pop right up out of the valley floor. One moment she was driving among the shade trees and the next moment she was in the city. Its quaint shops and restaurants followed one another through the entire main street until just as suddenly the surroundings changed and Abby found herself in the middle of a residential area. She made a u-turn and headed back to an Italian restaurant she had spotted as she drove through a few minutes before.

As she entered the Primo Italiano, heads turned and

patrons smiled. “Buon giorno. Come in, my dear and have a seat at our choicest table.”

It was a pleasant experience and Abby needed all the pleasant experiences she could get. After finishing the much needed warm meal, she paid the bill and checked the local phone book. The only Ranno listed was a Stan Ranno, no Donna Ranno. The address in the phone book looked similar to the one she had seen in Uncle Don’s file, so she decided to make an impromptu visit. *Maybe Donna is that Mrs. Stan Ranno.*

The sun was setting as Abby pulled into 2040 South Brightham. It was a modest but pleasant looking house with manicured yard and a large garden on the side. As she stood at the door waiting for someone to answer her knock, her knees almost gave out from under her. She had to hang on to the side rail of the front steps. *Maybe coming here wasn’t a good idea,* she thought and almost turned to run for her car.

Suddenly the door jerked open and a woman of about fifty-five stood before her. “Yes?” was the impatient query.

Abby spoke quickly as if expecting the woman to shut the door on her. “I’m looking for a woman known as Donna Ranno. Are you that woman?”

“Yes, I’m Donna. My husband is Stan. What can I do for you?” She answered wearily as if it was just another irritation she had to deal with in her day.

“Mrs. Ranno, I’m Abigail Demitt and I think we need to talk about an old warehouse in Deerburn and the family kept there. Maybe you have a room where we can speak more privately? I wouldn’t want to bother your family.”

The color drained from Donna’s face and for a moment it seemed she was going to faint. She looked furtively into her living room and then motioned for Abby to follow her. The sitting room was located near the front of the house and as they entered, Donna closed the door firmly. "Now, what are you doing here? Why did you have to bring that up? I want to forget all of that."

"*You* want to forget all that! What about my family? Don't you think they want to forget?" Abby shouted and was going to continue when Donna interrupted, "We can only talk a few minutes. My husband is around and I don't want him to know anything about my past. Now, get to the point and then please leave."

As Abby stood facing the woman who years before had been a true threat to her family, prickly jabs of apprehension filled her. It was only as she reminded herself that *she* was the one who had been maligned and whose whole life had been turned upside down by the doctor with whom Donna had collaborated, that she was able to continue.

"I had to see what kind of woman you were," Abby began. "I couldn't believe that any decent person could have been involved with the scheme that doctor had perpetrated. I need to know why you worked for him, and what you could possibly have gained from it. Then, I want you to tell me anything you can about my formation to life."

"You can't just come into my home and make demands on me," Donna whispered fearfully.

"I'm afraid I can," Abby bluffed, "I could call the police right now. I'm sure they'd be interested in my story." Though Abby knew she would never take that action, the words were enough to change Donna's attitude completely. The woman's face suddenly mirrored the years of shame and guilt she suffered. Tears formed in her eyes and she had to sit down to keep from collapsing.

Abby couldn't bluff anymore. "Donna, please help me...give me some answers. I need to know why I was formed, was it just for money? And more importantly, how was I formed? What kind of a future did that doctor think I would have, or didn't he even care?"

Donna was about to answer when there was a sharp, insistent knock at the door. "Donna, are you OK. Who've you got in there with you?"

"Stan, it's a young woman whose parents I used to know," Donna responded nervously. "She just stopped to say hello. We're just going to visit awhile."

Footsteps shuffled away from the door and Donna motioned to Abby. "Sit down, please. You ask me very difficult questions and you ask them after twenty years have passed. Many things I don't remember, or don't want to remember."

"I'm waiting," responded Abby quietly but firmly.

"Well, to my knowledge you were formed entirely in the lab from the DNA of Ruby...Cramden, I think her name was. Just how the doctor did it, I'm not sure, but using the DNA he was able to fertilize the egg in an entirely different manner than had ever been attempted before. It worked, obviously, and you gestated perfectly...ending up a prized baby. Dr. Nick had big plans for you. You were going to be his fame and fortune, but his plans didn't work out. I think he would have exploited you as his first human clone, probably for the rest of your life."

Donna had to stop and wipe her forehead with a tissue. "I think the doctor fully expected you to be a normal being, albeit a clone, and live a regular life. At least he never said anything to the contrary. Does that help?"

Abby wasn't sure what to say. It seemed like positive news, but certainly not as complete as she was hoping. "It helps, Donna, but I need to know more. Don't you understand, this is my life? I need to know who and just *what* I am for my own sanity. Is there anyone else you can remember who might be able to add more to what you've told me?"

Encouraged by Abby's sincere attitude, Donna began to relax. Now after all these years she was able to put a face to that cloned baby, and was beginning to understand the dilemma Abby must be experiencing. "The only one I can think of would be Dr. Minolo in Nortovia. He was handling the announcement part of the cloning and was interested in working with Dr. Nick further. I think they discussed the procedure and other things during their association. He might be able to help you if he's still alive."

Abby slowly stood and reached out her hand to Donna. "Thank you. I know this encounter must have been hard for you as well. If I may ask, what was your motive for working with that evil man? You don't seem to be the kind of person who would want to hurt people."

Donna looked directly into Abby's face and Abby knew it must have been a question Donna had asked herself hundreds of times over the years. *Why did she do it?*

"Miss Demitt, I wish I could answer that. Truthfully, I don't know what prompted me to take that job, or even once having that job, what prompted me to continue with the doctor when I realized what he was doing."

Abby watched the woman question herself and try to find reasons.

Donna continued in a monotone as if talking to herself, "I was just married after a terrible divorce at the time and was deeply in debt. Money. I'm sure money was the first reason I even thought about working in that underground warehouse laboratory." Then she lowered her eyes and spoke in whispered tones. "Power. I hate to admit it, but I enjoyed the power the job gave me."

Abby found anger welling up inside. "Well, what about my parents and my brothers the doctor had imprisoned there. Didn't that bother you?"

That question brought Donna out of her reverie and she looked defeated. "Of course that bothered me. I'm not inhuman. But, the doctor had such convincing reasons for his actions that eventually I just wanted to believe him, so I did. At least I told myself I believed him. I think I was mesmerized by him and his lofty plans. After all, I would have been famous too. You know what I mean?"

So evil is catching, thought Abby as she watched the woman's self-realization, then self-loathing and finally self-pardon. *How can I judge her? In many ways she's a pawn of the infamous doctor, and maybe after our visit she'll try to work this out in her life as well.*

"You've been straight with me and for that I thank you," Abby responded. "I can't understand how being famous or even being mesmerized by the doctor could be excuses for your part in the plan to hold me and my family hostage, but I have a feeling that after today, you will be doing a lot of self-analyzing."

She walked toward the door but couldn't leave until she expressed the thought that had just come to mind. "Donna, I'm a Christian, and because of God's love for me, I am able to have love for others, even when it doesn't seem possible. As we've talked, I think in some ways you've gone through a trauma because of this too, and I want you to know that I forgive you. I know God will forgive you too if you ask him...and then maybe you'll be able to forgive yourself."

With that Abby found her way out the front door to her car, leaving Donna alone with tears trickling down her face. *Forgive myself? Maybe someday, with help?*

Chapter Seventeen

Abby took a minute to compose herself as she mulled over the events she had experienced in that short time. Two of the people involved in her background were unhappy and suffering in some way themselves. Poor Arthur...a lost life because of his bad choices, and Donna...full of guilt at once being a part of something with such unknown consequences.

She sighed deeply as if the air she inhaled would fill her with a new existence and exhaling would eliminate the shadow holding her so tightly. Her thoughts were interrupted by the ringing of her cell phone. She glanced down and saw it was David calling. With a shaking hand she reached down to turn it off. He had been calling her often since she had left Vesta, but she never answered...there was no future for them. Even though he loved her, how could he ever understand that she was a...she wouldn't even think of that awful word and she shut her mind off just as she had shut off her phone. Starting the engine she headed toward the outskirts of Rutheford to look for a motel.

Sleep didn't come easily for Abby and when it did, she dreamed of David. His face appeared as real as if he was with her. The look of love he had for her prompted tears to fall and she awoke sobbing into her pillow. Once awakened with the memory of her love, sleep evaded her for hours. She tossed and turned, took an aspirin, watched the clock, and finally dropped to her knees. "Jesus, I don't understand this. Why did you even bring David into my life if I was to find out about my unbelievable beginning? I want to trust you and know that you will get me through this, but it is so hard. Please help me!"

She sat down on the floor by the bed recalling once again the agonizing questions about her relationship with God. *Does God even hear my prayers if I'm not a normal human? Why would he allow this to happen if I was really his?* Then the question that brought tears and panic, *Will I go to heaven when I die because I believe in Jesus? Or is there no place for a clone? God didn't form me, did he? I'm just an experiment!*

Finally, that still small voice she had heard so often during her life seemed to speak to her, "Be calm, there is much more for you to know."

David had fallen asleep in his armchair. He hadn't had a normal night's sleep since he was called about Abby's hospitalization. He often sat up reading until he fell asleep. He had been sleeping fitfully about an hour when Abby seemed to appear before him. She was there, holding out her hand to him and smiling that breathtaking smile. He called her name and reached for her, but his book fell from his hands to the floor and he awoke with a start.

"Oh Abby!" he cried into the darkness. "Where are you? If you'd just call me, I'd come to you in a minute."

A dark night. A sleepless night. Yet two hearts were together even if only in unanswered cries.

Chapter Eighteen

As the two dreams continued, hundreds of miles from Abby in the country of Nortovia, a woman walked the early morning streets of Semsk, one of the modest farming villages several miles from Zenova, the capital city. She made it a habit to venture out before the village came to life.

The villagers referred to her as "that mysterious lady," and after many years, that was all the recognition she wanted. She arrived at the market just as the farmers were unfurling their awnings and setting up their luscious fruits and vegetables.

As was her habit, she walked to the first booth, smiled at the man organizing the produce and added her vegetables to the table. Her garden had grown over the years and she now had a good supply of produce to bring each week, after which she was paid a percentage of the profits.

Before leaving, she selected a few items of fruit, breads and fresh pork or chicken from the farmers. By the time she had visited all the booths, and picked up the money from the previous week's sale, she was supplied again until the next week.

"Mr. Jafft," she nodded toward one of the men as she finished her purchase and moved on. "Good apples today, Mrs. Norman." She was pleasant but aloof, and although she had come almost every week to the market for as long as anyone could remember, no one really knew her. They just accepted her and responded with like pleasantries.

At first glance, one might think the mysterious lady was an average looking woman, but at closer look her beauty would be noticeable. Though nearing fifty years of age, her stature was that of a young woman, and if she had worn her hair down without her usual scarf, the filtering of grey would not have hidden the vibrant color that was still there.

"Nice day," the mysterious woman acknowledged to two farmer's wives as they got out of their truck. They both smiled amiably and turned to watch her walk toward the edge of town and the country road that would take her to her farm house.

"She's mysterious all right," the larger of the two women said. "All those years and we don't know her any better than when she first came here."

"That's certain," the other wife answered. "I kind of wish we could know her better. She seems nice. I wonder why she doesn't want any friends."

"I don't know...maybe it has something to do with her arrival here in Semsk. Remember how strange that was? That doctor brought her here to help with his ailing mother. Poor Emma, she only lived five years after that. Now *she* lives there...that mysterious one."

"I remember that," the conversation continued. "After she came we didn't see her for weeks, and when she finally came to town she didn't seem to be doing very well. She walked with crutches and wore those silly sunglasses to cover the black eyes she had. I wonder if she was beat up or fell or something."

"Boy, I'd sure like to know her story."

Both women stood watching for a moment longer shaking their heads, and then turned their attention to the crowd gathering at the market.

Chapter Nineteen

Abby awoke after a fitful night and groped her way to the small coffee pot on the counter in the still dark motel room. After fixing the four cups allowed, she showered, and dressed in one of the two pant suits she had taken time to bring with her.

She sat in numbed silence at the small table in her room glancing out at the purple haze surrounding the mountains. She slowly sipped the welcome cup of coffee while concentrating on the list of names from Uncle Don.

Now where do I go? What's next for me in this search? I learned some important things from Donna Ranno so it wasn't a fruitless visit. We were able to face each other and be honest with each other. I'm thankful I was able to forgive her.

Arthur is another story. I'm so glad I met him. I learned things about Ruby that only he could tell me, and...I like him. I really like him.

She crossed off Arthur's name on the list and then Donna's as she tried to decipher the numerous notes she had scribbled at Uncle Don's. *Can't quite figure this name out...Menalo? No, let's see it looks more like Minolo. That's right, he's that doctor in Nortovia that was setting up the events of the big announcement. Big announcement for them...but not for me. I wonder if they ever thought what it would be like for me.*

Abby decided Nortovia would be her next stop, but it was a long trip and she was still far from her quest for information. She made flight reservations to leave that evening. That would give her enough time to drive to New York from Rutheford. She quickly gathered her belongings and headed her car south for the next chapter in her search, which would prove to be the most intriguing by far.

Thoughts of Abby were on David's mind as he sat in his office trying to imagine where she was and what she was doing. Abby was in Josh's lingering thoughts when he should have been thinking of his sermon notes, and Stephen had to put down his morning paper as thoughts of Abby took precedence.

LaGuardia terminal was a mass of humanity running, walking, milling around. The pitch of so many voices was almost unbearable for Abby as she sat waiting for an electric cart to transport her to her gate. Though she was surrounded by hundreds of people in the terminal she felt completely and utterly alone. Even if she would have had someone to talk to, she could never share the horror inside. Her thoughts drifted to her mother and the family's plight twenty years ago that Sarah had revealed.

Mother must have waited in this same airport with me to board her flight to Nortovia too. It must have been terrible for her knowing about me and then having to leave Dad and the boys to go to a place where those awful people were going to exploit me. "Oh Mom," Abby whispered quietly as she reached for her tissues. Her tears came easily these days.

I wonder how mom and dad felt when they heard the news about me. It must have pained them all through the years, but they always loved me dearly and never let on that there was any problem. Abby's mind was boggled by all the events of that time years ago. *Dad imprisoned with Josh and Stephen, Mom having to take me to that foreign country where I was to become a specimen of man's triumph over morality, Ruby kidnapping me with Mom in pursuit and that awful man chasing us. It must have been a nightmare of desperate shadows for them.*

Abby was so lost in her thoughts she almost missed the cart that had stopped in front of her. She exchanged a few words with the driver, but when they reached her gate and she left the cart, the overwhelming thoughts continued to punish her. As the boarding started, she mechanically handed the attendant her boarding pass and walked down the ramp to the plane as if she was a wind-up toy that had begun to wind down. Once she was seated and fastened her seat belt, she was unable to remember how she had even gotten to her seat.

While Abby sat in the crowded jet for her flight to Nortovia, Stephen and Tiffany seated themselves awkwardly in the marriage counselor's office. Tiffany had tears in her eyes and Stephen was nervous and jumpy.

"Let's start with a brief word of prayer," Matt Peterson encouraged. "It's best to begin with God's help."

After the prayer Tiffany shifted uncomfortably. She wasn't used to prayer, and especially not in a setting like this. She'd never thought much about God and his Son Jesus, and never thought much about life after death either. That was a subject she wanted to avoid. "Could we get this started?" she said somewhat impatiently.

Stephen turned to look at her, but she kept looking straight ahead. "It won't take long, Tiff, and hopefully we can learn some things that'll help us."

The counselor cleared his throat, shuffled his papers and the session began.

Chapter Twenty

The flight to Nortovia seemed endless as Abby tried to figure out some kind of plan for her search there. Who should she see first...the police? Maybe she should find that Dr. Minolo first and talk to him. She slept fitfully between the barraging thoughts or dreams in which vivid pictures of familiar faces appeared and then disappeared.

Sweet Sarah...what would Abby have done without her love and strength all during her life, but especially after her mother and father were killed. Sarah's face morphed into Abby's mother's face. Dorie had never lost her youthful beauty or her loving devotion to her husband and children.

Her father's face appeared and quickly interchanged with that of Stephen and Josh, all laughing over some silly joke or prank they pulled. Uncle Don's face was there in the background of her mini dreams, and someone else's face from her past kept pushing forward, but Abby didn't know who it was. It was a woman's face, a woman with bright red hair and eyes just like Abby, but every time Abby tried to visualize the face better, it disappeared again.

The cabin attendant tapped Abby softly on the shoulder to remind her that the plane would be landing soon and all seat belts had to be fastened. "Miss Demitt, I thought you'd like to know that English is spoken by many of the Nortovian people, especially those in the professions dealing with tourism. They're not all fluent in English, but do understand it and usually speak it fairly well."

Abby thanked her, leaving her dream world for the reality of the moment, but the illusive person in her dream with the vivid red hair wouldn't leave her mind. Then as she buckled her seat belt and leaned back to look out the window, it dawned on her…that face must be Ruby's. *Of course, it has to be…the red hair and eyes so much like mine. It must be what Ruby had looked like in my childhood memories.* "Why couldn't I have gotten to know you?" she whispered out loud as the plane landed effortlessly on the tarmac in Nortovia.

The customs and security people at Nortovia's main terminal were thorough. As one of the personnel frisked Abby, the officer apologized and commented that their security had gotten extremely tight since the many terroristic threats in the world. "Ten, twenty years ago, we hardly even looked at the checked luggage. Things are sure different here now."

Once through the security gate, Abby lost no time in finding a taxi to take her to the hotel. She needed some time to sort out her thoughts and make the appropriate plans.

The Nortovia Ambassador Arms Hotel was swanky, at least to Abby's less sophisticated mind. The artwork was minimal but tastefully placed throughout the lobby. Computers were discreetly situated on the many French Provincial tables so not to disturb the elegance of the room, but still afford their patrons the latest in electronic equipment.

Abby's room was the style every young woman would want in her home. The décor was rich in whites, tans and black which blended charmingly with the white carved furniture. Once she spotted the large bed's overstuffed mattress and throw pillows, she decided she would try to enjoy it even though she wasn't on a pleasure trip by any means.

After luxuriously lounging on the comfortable bed, she unpacked her overnight bag and put her few pieces of clothing in the drawer of the dresser. She wished she had put more thought into her wardrobe before leaving, but it was too late for that. *I'll just mix and match what I have and hope that will do. Who knows how long I'll even be here?*

The hotel and the posh room gave her a brief sense of normalcy until Abby sat at the desk and emptied her purse. There confronting her were the notes she had jotted down from Uncle Don's files. The dark shadow that had taken its place in her life seemed an almost invisible ghost as she reread the notes. There was no escaping the problem…the elegant room in the famous hotel couldn't erase the reason she had come to Nortovia.

The first name that jumped out at her was Dr. Luis Minolo. He was the biochemist working with Dr. Nick on Project A, of which she was the central figure. She had a goal of finding out the who-what-when-where and why of her identity, yet the pain involved with what she might learn sent waves of nausea through her. Hesitantly she dialed the number she had found in the phonebook next to Luis Minolo and almost hoped there would be no answer. But in a few short rings a man's voice came on the line.

"Dr. Minolo here," the doctor answered professionally in case it was a company seeking his expertise in biological research.

Abby's voice responded in a distinct American accent. "Doctor, I'm visiting Nortovia and as I've heard so many interesting things about you, I'd like to chat with you a few minutes at your earliest convenience."

Dr. Minolo leaned back in his chair warmed by his apparent notoriety. He was no longer the weak, frail man who twenty years earlier had worked with the infamous Dr. Nick. He had put on an attractive amount of weight, and to work off his frustration at the depressing failure of their project, he began a weight lifting program. He had become a rather handsome man, much more at peace than before he became involved with the cloning project. At that time he had been so sure the announcement of the first human clone creation would make him famous as well, but that was before the child had disappeared and all the dreams ended abruptly.

His voice became more authoritative as he answered, “Of course. I’d be most happy to chat with…what did you say your name was?”

“It’s Abby, and thank you for consenting to see me. Would tomorrow afternoon be convenient for you?”

“It’s a date,” he responded in his most charming manner. “My office is in the Superior Office Complex on Third Avenue. See you at say, 3:00 tomorrow.”

When the conversation ended, Abby noticed her hands were shaking. At last she was going to talk to one of the pivotal figures from her past, and she was nervous. What would she find out?

Chapter Twenty-one

As Abby took a nap of exhausted sleep in Nortovia, Stephen was unable to sleep in the dark of the night in New York. He slipped out of bed and sat by the window thinking about the counseling session that afternoon. Dr. Peterson had begun in a non-intrusive manner which helped to put Tiffany at ease. And, when Tiffany was more at ease, the whole situation was better.

Stephen had carefully voiced his thoughts on their marriage trouble and then Tiffany was given equal time. She hesitated and shook her head as if to give up. "I don't know what to say," she had said despondently. "Something just happened to our love somewhere along the way, and I don't know how to get it back. Actually, I don't know at this point if I *want* to get it back."

Stephen remembered how he had stared at her in disbelief. When she first told him that, he thought she was just being emotional, but now as she repeated the fact she didn't even know if she wanted to love him, it was devastating.

Dr. Peterson was taking notes and as their first session ended, he looked up, "We will want to spend more time than we have left today on the feelings Tiffany just expressed. That will be the area we'll focus on first at our next session. Do you both agree?"

Stephen nodded and Tiffany just looked ahead blankly until Dr. Peterson prodded her. "Would you agree, Tiffany?"

"Oh, I guess so," she answered absently.

The session had ended as Dr. Peterson handed them each a schedule of continued visits. Tiffany looked up at Stephen. "You didn't say we'd have to keep coming after the first couple visits. Was that a trick to get me here?"

Stephen couldn't believe his ears. What had happened to his wife in the last few years that had made her so hard and inflexible? "Trick, what do you mean trick?" he said as he opened the door for her. He instinctively grabbed for her arm to help her down the stairs but she deliberately walked several steps ahead of him. *So it's come to this,* Stephen thought sadly.

On Sunday, the day after Josh and Cindy's discovery of their mutual interest in each other, Josh delivered the first of several sermons about people's reactions to those society considers outcasts. He spotted Cindy right away sitting near the front and gazing at him intently. It disarmed him, so he glanced around the congregation as he spoke rather than concentrate on her…although concentrating on Cindy was easy for him to do.

He began his sermon describing society as they all knew it. He talked about those whose lives appear to be "normal" and those who are different mentally, physically and spiritually. His congregation settled in to listen as Josh spoke with a strange new passion, questioning, "Ask yourselves how you would treat a person you see who is different in some way?" The congregation squirmed; some seriously reflecting and a few smugly sure they had no problem accepting everyone.

Josh continued. "And think carefully, what would your reaction be to a genetically engineered person, or even a person who was, say, a human clone?"

A few titters of laughter were heard, but the majority of the congregation sat in absolute silence wondering what their true reaction would be.

Josh then spoke quietly and earnestly as if in an intimate conversation with each person, "God has reassured us over and over again in Scripture that he deeply loves each of us. So, think about it, if God loves us even though we're sinful people, don't you think we have a responsibility to love others regardless of differences? We are all creations of God no matter *how* we were created. By our treatment of those who are unlike us, God could get a pretty good idea of our values. Do we think of ourselves as God's *better* creations?"

That question seemed to have a profound effect on the majority present as Josh related it back to the Bible by quoting Leviticus 19:18, King James Version, "Thou shalt love thy neighbor as thyself." To affirm that truth, Josh also quoted from 1John 4:7, 8, "Beloved, let us love one another: for love is of God; and every one that loveth is born of God, and knoweth God. He that loveth not knoweth not God; for God is love."

The silence in the church was convicting. Josh paused briefly and continued, "As I close today, I'd like each of you to go home and sometime this week study John 1 verses 12 and 13 in the New International Version of the Bible: "Yet to all who received him, to those who believed in his name, he gave the right to become children of God — children born not of natural descent, nor of human decision or a husband's will, but born of God."

As the lesson closed, there were few if any of Josh's parishioners who doubted the truth of God's love, or who doubted how God would have his loved ones treated according to his standards. The only doubts that might have crept into their minds were doubts as to whether they could follow those standards implicitly.

Josh watched Cindy as he finished the Scripture quotation and she was nodding her own "Amen."

Afterward as he stood at the door shaking hands with his parishioners, many expressed an interest in hearing a continuation of the subject. Toward the end of the exiting crowd Cindy came up to him and warmly shook his hand. "It was wonderful to hear you. You truly have a gift. It was as though you had a personal relationship with someone considered an outcast," she looked at him quizzically hoping he might answer, but he only smiled.

"Cindy, if you'd like to wait a few minutes, maybe we could have Sunday dinner together at one of Vesta's famous eating establishments?"

Cindy wouldn't admit it even to herself, but she had been hoping Josh would ask her to join him and she nodded eagerly. *I hope I wasn't too eager,* she thought as she tried unsuccessfully to calm the growing excitement she felt at the prospect of dinner with him.

Josh also felt an excitement to be with Cindy, and as he shook hands with the remaining people, he was distracted by thoughts of her.

Chapter Twenty-two

As the taxi sped through the city of Zenova, Abby's thoughts were jumbled and her nerves frayed. Dr. Minolo was a key player in this horrific event and now she was about to meet him. What would she even say to him? He must know all about her…that she's a…*clone. I'm scared of what I'll find out. I don't know how much I can handle. Oh, dear God, this is so awful!* "I hate this!" she said out loud and the cab driver turned, "You say something, Lady?"

"Nothing," was the reply. *But I do hate this,* she thought to herself.

Her stomach fluttered as the cab stopped in front of the Superior Office Complex and she glanced at the ominous looking grey metal doors. No windows appeared in sight until about the 12th floor. She paid the cab driver and walked hesitantly into the building, forcing herself to put one foot in front of the other until she approached the reception desk. Dr. Minolo's office was on the 14th floor.

The elevator was manually operated by a gentle little man with thick glasses and a large smile. "You're goin' to see the doc, huh?" he said with a thick accent, pushing the lever to begin the assent. "He's good guy, that Dr. Minolo. You know him?"

Abby was surprised at all the questions from a complete stranger, but tried to be pleasant despite her fear of the visit. "I don't know him but I'm sure he's a nice person," was her only reply. The fourteenth floor couldn't come soon enough. *I need to get this over with. Oh God, why is there always this awful shadow following me?*

At the fourteenth floor, Abby exchanged smiles with the pleasant elevator operator and headed down the long corridor to find the door to the doctor's office. That was easy enough to do as his name was painted in large letters covering the majority of space on the door window.

Cautiously she opened the door and was instantly greeted with a firm handshake by no other than the doctor himself. "Hello I'm Dr. Minolo. Do come in. My secretary is out ill today."

The offices were somewhat dark so as they entered his private office he let go of her hand and walked over to the window. "Let me pull the shades open so we can see each other better. The sun loves this room at this time of day."

Abby found the nearest chair to the desk and looked up as Dr. Minolo turned from the window and saw her clearly for the first time. His face turned ashen as he gasped, "Oh my…Oh my!"

Abby was stunned. She turned around to look behind her in case he had seen something else in the room. "What is it?" she asked apprehensively.

Dr. Minolo tried to gain some composure as he sat down at his desk searching for an appropriate answer. After a long pause he managed, "You look so much like someone I knew once that it just took me by surprise. I guess now would be a good time for introductions. What is your name, and what can I do for you?"

Well this is it, thought Abby as she plunged in and hoped for the best. "My name is Abigail Demitt. From what I've read, you probably know me better as 'Project A.' We actually met twenty years ago when my mother and I were forced to come to Nortovia with Dr. Nick Krebsny and his group…do you remember?"

How could I forget, thought the doctor. "Twenty years is a long time. I do remember Dr. Nick and his research lab in Deerburn. The rest is rather hazy."

"Hazy! Hazy! How can you be so apathetic! I'm 'Project A', the most important thing Dr. Nick worked on, as I understand. How can you not remember? This is my life here...you had a part in that terrible experiment. You have to remember!" By this time Abby was flushed and the tears had begun to run down her cheeks. "Have you no heart?"

Dr. Minolo stared at the young woman in front of him...the young woman who was almost identical to Ruby. Of course he remembered, but he never thought he'd ever see Abigail Demitt or even hear of her again, and now here she was in his office expecting answers to questions he dreaded. Here was the very clone who had been so important to all of them, sitting across from him, but there was no hope now of ever revealing her to the world. Cloning was now illegal in Nortovia and all the papers and proof had been destroyed in that horrible fire in Deerburn.

His handsome face mirrored sadness as he slowly responded, "I remember. Yes, I remember. It was to be a celebratory time in all our lives and instead turned out to be a disaster. You and your mother disappeared and ended up in the United States again and I was left with the bills and remnants of a glorious dream."

"You talk about it as if it was only a difficult time in your life. What about me? Have you ever, *ever* thought about whether I'd find out about being a clone, and just how it would affect me? Have you ever stopped to realize what an abnormal thing it is to clone a human being, or were you only thinking of yourself?" Abby was angered and wasn't about to let this man get by with his pitiful whining about his loss. Her loss was irrevocable...it was her very life, her very existence.

"I'm truly sorry. You have a right to be upset. I shouldn't have been so thoughtless. Perhaps we can begin again on a better basis?"

Abby relented, but mostly because she was unaccustomed to being rude to anyone. "Yes, let's begin again. I came here to see you in the hopes you would be able to give me some technical and biological information about my history. It's desperately important to me that I learn all I can. It's the only way I will be able to survive as a *clone.*"

Dr. Minolo's thoughts had briefly gone to the woman who so long ago had taken his heart. "Abigail, before I begin to tell you, I must have your promise that you will never reveal anything you hear from me. Since the time of the planned announcement of your cloning twenty years ago, Nortovia has passed strict rules against human cloning, and both you and I could get into a lot of trouble if any of this got out. Anyway ..." he continued, "I'm sure you don't want the world to know you are a clone, do you?"

"Of course not! Then I would really feel like a freak!"

The doctor was quick to respond to Abby's remark, "My dear, you are *not* a freak just because you are a clone. You must not think of yourself that way. Try to think of yourself as a 'successful medical breakthrough.'"

Abby settled back in her chair and tried to be calm as she listened to information that would hopefully help establish some kind of identity. "A medical breakthrough? Why tamper with life as it was meant to be? Who gave you two doctors the right to play God?"

"Miss Demitt, I was not playing God, neither are any of my scientific colleagues. We just...well, let's just say we see things differently." Dr. Minolo nervously ran his hands through his thick graying hair.

"When Dr. Nick first contacted me with his plan and asked for my assistance in the announcement part of it, Nortovia had no laws against cloning. You had been 'born,' so to speak the first time he called me and you were at the Montgomery Agency being cared for by a special nurse."

"But Doctor, I want to know *how* I was formed," Abby cried. "Can you explain it so I can understand it?"

How do I tell her without making her feel worse? "Let me try," he responded nervously. "First, Dr. Nick had to get someone to supply the DNA for the cloning, and that person turned out to be a Ruby Cramden, but I'm sure you know that. Once they had her DNA, the doctor used his unique formula to coach the cells to reproduce as if the cells had been fertilized."

"So I have no 'father'?"

"No, Abigail, not in the biological sense of 'father.'" As he could see she was starting to unravel, he continued quickly, "Then the doctor grew the fetus, you of course, to maturity in a simulated womb right there in the lab until the gestation period of nine months was complete. It was another breakthrough. By gestating you in the simulated womb they were able to watch your entire growth process."

Abby *was* unraveling and with tears in her eyes she almost shouted at him, "Fetus? Simulated womb? Gestation period? Do you understand you are talking about ***me***? I am not just an experiment, I am someone!" And as she spoke those words, she stopped. Her spirits strangely lifted as she thought, *I said it myself...I am someone. I'm not just an experiment...I am some one!*

Dr. Minolo purposely ignored her outburst and continued as if he hadn't heard her. "Dr. Nick was an absolute genius in human engineering. And, as I look at you I am more convinced of his genius than ever. You are perfect, beautiful and appear to be quite intelligent. It's a shame he couldn't have seen you as you are today. That explosion at his lab ruined a lot of things for a lot of people."

Abby had been trying to assimilate all that she was hearing, but when Dr. Minolo spoke so highly of the infamous doctor, she couldn't stand it. "Have you no idea what a horrible man he was? He kept my whole family imprisoned while he forced us to Nortovia under threats of death. He was evil!"

"Yes, I know that. He was evil, but he was also, however, a genius in his field. I didn't literally mean that he should be here. He was an unfeeling egotist who destroyed many people in his wake. But I know of no one since who has even come close to his discoveries in cloning."

Dr. Minolo did appear to be truly sorry for glamorizing such an infamously evil man and decided in the future he should keep those opinions to himself.

Abby decided to ignore his last statement and continued, "Tell me what you know about our time here twenty years ago."

Dr. Minolo walked over to the hot plate on his console. "Would you like some fresh hot coffee? Maybe we can take a break for a few minutes and let you digest what I've been able to tell you so far."

"Actually I don't care for coffee now, and I would like to continue our discussion," Abby responded impatiently.

The doctor poured a cup of the hot black liquid for himself and resigned to continue the conversation as he sat back in his chair. "I met you all at the air terminal on your arrival. Your mother was holding you. She was a lovely and gracious person, although I didn't get a chance to know her. Ruby Cramden was there. It seemed she was helping your mother take care of you."

"Who else was there besides that…doctor?"

"Well, with Dr. Nick was his assistant Rhonda, along with Duke, the doctor's bodyguard as we all referred to him, though we knew he was much more than that. He was a mean one, and the one who pursued Ruby Cramden when she took you out of the hotel. He also pursued your mother when she found you and tried to escape with you.

"You probably know the rest...Duke shot Ruby and she shot and winged him as she fell. Then you and your mother escaped, ended up in a church and eventually got to the airport to fly home. I don't have any other details to give you even though I realize it's all quite bizarre."

Abby had been gesturing the last few minutes to ask a question and when the doctor stopped, she spoke up immediately. "What about Ruby? I assume she died, but whatever happened to her body?"

That was the question Dr. Minolo was not ready to answer. "I'm afraid I can't answer any questions about Ruby. I'm sorry, but I hope our conversation has helped you to understand the events that happened all those years ago."

Abby responded resolutely, "Even though it's devastating for me to think of myself as the result of an experiment, you have given me more insight into how I was…formed." She wiped away a tear. "But I still need to know about Ruby. In some ways I am part of her and I've just got to know what happened to her. If you know, please tell me. Is she buried somewhere here in Zenova?" Abby was persistent, but getting nowhere.

"Abigail, I truly can't tell you anything about Ruby, but let me have your cell number and I'll contact you if I think of any more to tell you."

Abby handed the doctor her number, and was walking toward the door when Dr. Minolo cleared his throat. "Miss Demitt, I cannot let you leave without telling you the truth about Ruby Cramden."

Abigail turned expectantly, only to hear the words she had secretly hoped she'd never hear. "Ruby Cramden is dead. I'm sorry to have to tell you this. I wanted to spare you, but I think you have a right to know."

Abigail reached for the nearest chair and held on. "Dead? She really is dead then? I guess I knew that…it's just so final to hear it spoken." She burst into tears of hopelessness and anger. "How did she die? Was it when she was shot by that awful bodyguard Duke?"

The doctor sat on the edge of his desk and explained, "After she was shot and Duke left to follow you and your mother, she managed to crawl and stumble her way out of that building. She only made it as far as a clump of bushes, and it was there that Duke found her dead later that evening. He took her body and disposed of it…I'm sorry but I don't know how or where."

Abby gave up fighting her emotions and let despair wash over her. It was moments before she was composed enough to leave Dr. Minolo's office and head back to her car.

Chapter Twenty-three

A few days after the counseling session that had disturbed Tiffany and puzzled Stephen, he drove into the driveway of his tutor home in New York after a tedious work day. He was surprised to see that Tiffany's car was gone, especially since the boys would be home from baseball practice any minute. He waved to Mrs. Bradley next door who gestured that she had been watching for the boys, but they hadn't gotten home yet. It was good to have her nearby to help out. Even though she was in her sixties, she was an able and responsible neighbor, always ready to help out when his schedule and Tiffany's conflicted and they weren't able to be home when the boys were dropped off after practice.

As he opened the door from the garage to the house he saw the school bus at the curb and within minutes heard the usual exuberant salutation from his boys. Even though they were eight, they still enjoyed hugging him and playfully boxing him when he came home from work. He looked forward to it enthusiastically.

"Do you know where Mom might have gone, boys? Her car is gone." Stephen's casual question brought "don't know" from the boys as they scampered up to their rooms to change into their jeans. Stephen put his briefcase on the kitchen table and called Tiffany's name several times just in case her car was in the shop and she might be home. He was about to check upstairs when he walked through the living room and spotted an envelope propped against a candle on the fireplace mantle. It was in Tiffany's writing and Stephen opened it apprehensively.

"Stephen," the letter began, "I can't go on pretending any longer. I don't love you and haven't loved you for a long time. I only stayed because of the boys, but I'm convinced they need you more than they need me. I am leaving them in your custody. I saw a lawyer this morning and made those provisions. I'm going on an extended trip and I won't be back. I've written a note to each of the boys assuring them that I love them. The notes are in our safe deposit box to be given them when you see fit. I'm sorry, Stephen, but it's over. Tiffany."

Stephen was incredulous. *She hasn't loved me for a long time? She never told me or even wanted to talk about any problems.* "Oh, God, how am I going to get through this? I love her, and she's the mother of our boys." Stephen wept bitterly, trying to keep the sound of his sobs from the boys upstairs. After he calmed down, he slumped down on the leather couch until the darkness filtered through the windows and dimmed the room. He was unable to think of anything beyond that moment.

"Hey Dad, how come you're sitting in the dark? When're we gonna eat?" Jason asked as Jeremy came over to Stephen to see what was wrong. "Have you been crying, Dad? What's the deal?" Both boys were now standing in front of him expecting an answer and after that expecting their dinner.

"Boys, I don't know just how to tell you, but your mother has left us."

"Will she be home later, Dad?" the boys asked in unison.

Stephen knew the boys couldn't be fooled by made up stories, so he tried to be honest yet sensitive. "Jason, Jeremy, come sit down by me on the couch. I'm sure you want me to be honest with you. You're so grown up now that you are able to handle some bad news, aren't you?"

The boys nodded hesitantly wondering what was coming.

"Your mother loves you both very much, but the problem is she doesn't love me and she doesn't want to live with me anymore."

Jeremy and Jason each shook their heads as they kept repeating, "No. No."

Stephen hugged them both and the three of them sat close together while he tried to explain. "You must always remember that your mother loves you, but she has some problems that keep her from being here. I'll try my best to keep us a family. Think we can work together on that?"

The boys nodded when suddenly Jeremy looked up at Stephen and through his tears said softly, "Dad, I don't think Mom wanted to be here. She didn't want to come to our games or even do our homework with us."

"Yah," added Jason wiping his eyes, "she just didn't seem to want to be with us much. Maybe she just wanted to be by herself. She used to say that sometimes, didn't she, Jeremy?"

Jeremy agreed sadly. Stephen was amazed that the boys hadn't told him this before. "I didn't know that. Why didn't you say something to me about it?"

"We thought you'd get mad and then maybe she would really leave. But now she went anyway." Jason spoke for both of them.

Stephen hugged them closer and whispered to each of them how much he loved them and how he would take good care of them. "It'll take awhile but we'll get along, just the three of us, won't we? Let's start by having the biggest hamburger we can get at the Malt Shop. What do you say to that?"

The boys got up, walking slowly over to the foyer to grab their jackets and the three of them left huddled together as if to absorb all the love they could from each other.

Josh couldn't believe what his brother was telling him as they talked that evening on the phone. "Tiffany left? Just left you, the boys and everything? That seems impossible."

He listened attentively as his brother poured out his heart. To Josh, Stephen was supposed to be strong at times like this, but that would be difficult for any man under these conditions. Stephen sobbed for his sister Abby and the unbelievable news she had to endure, and now this terrible news about Tiffany. He couldn't get it together until Josh offered to leave immediately for New York to be with him for a few days.

In Nortovia, Dr. Minolo all but ran out of his office after his conversation with Abigail. He headed his car through rush hour traffic to the farmhouse in Semsk that had become so dear to him and the woman who had made it so.

My precious love, he thought anxiously. *Your memory has failed you all these years and now fragments of remembrances and glimmers of hope for you are returning. If all the repressed memories return it may be a beginning of hope for you but it could mean an ending of our relationship.* His thoughts kept his mind busy until he slowly pulled onto the gravel road of the farmhouse and noticed the picturesque smoke curls coming out of the brick chimney.

As he stepped up to the door she was there smiling, waiting for his familiar greeting. "Matushka, my dear."

Chapter Twenty-four

Abby was an emotional mess when she reached her car in the parking lot. *Ruby's dead. I know that for sure now and any hopes I had of having some kind of relationship with her is gone forever.* In her discouragement she mechanically started her car and headed into traffic. *I had been secretly hoping that by some miracle Ruby would be alive...I should have known better.*

She tried to focus on the information she had gotten from Dr. Minolo and what it meant in her search. *So now I know I was formed in an experiment for profit and fame, coaching the cells in just the perfect way to form some biological miracle! Then, as if that wasn't enough, they allowed me to grow in a simulated womb right there in the laboratory. Right there in the lab! I can't even imagine it.*

The sound of the motor and the soft music on the radio calmed her somewhat and she was able to think of some positive things that had come out of her visit with the doctor. *"Well...Dr. Minolo said I wasn't a freak. I guess that's positive...maybe. He did say I appeared to be perfect and that the doctor who created me would be proud of his 'work.' And then there is my realization that I am someone, not just a scientific experiment."*

Those thoughts quieted her spirit in a small way, but as she exited in the direction of her hotel, she realized that in spite of all she had learned from Dr. Minolo, at the moment she was saddest to learn about Ruby.

She had purposely driven through the area of the city where so much had happened to her family twenty years before. Thoughts of her mother brought her to the point of tears. *I miss her so much, and now Ruby is lost to me as well.*

She pulled over to the curb to check her map. *Where is that street?* Earlier she had marked the street with a felt pen in case she decided she had to renew those memories, no matter how painful. Sarah had said that Abby's mother specifically recalled Building #1400, and it was there that Ruby had taken shelter with Abby. Fortunately, Abby was only two at the time and couldn't remember what happened in the room at the front that held so much horror.

Abby found the Boulevard and the Savoy Hotel where the group had stayed. Starting at the hotel she drove down the street searching the buildings until she found #1400. When she got to the building she noticed it wasn't yellow any more as Sarah had described. It was painted red, but there was no mistaking it from the description she had gotten. She stopped her car in front of the building and closed her eyes as she tried to imagine what had happened there. *They were in this very building being threatened by that evil man and both Mom and Ruby tried to shield me from him.*

As she sat rigid and unable to relax, a thought came to her.

The police station! Maybe they would have some kind of report from twenty years ago that would indicate what happened in that building. Maybe they would even know if Ruby's body was ever recovered.

Consulting her street map of Zenova once again, Abby found the location of the nearest police precinct. On her arrival she was surprised at the attractive architecture of the building. It looked as if it had recently been sand polished. Once inside, however, she realized it was just a normal police station with the usual bustling commotion and paper mess.

Abby spoke to several policemen before finding one who was able to help her with the old police records. One officer signaled her that he would help and she accompanied him to the records library where he diligently examined the several fiches from twenty years earlier. He was able to determine that some kind of disturbance had been reported in Building #1400 on the Boulevard, but the attending officers found nothing to warrant further investigation. They reported holes found in the walls, but they were scraped clean of any contamination. Due to lack of evidence, the reported incident was closed.

"The officers didn't find any wounded people there?" Abby asked anxiously, but the report was read back to her.

"Nothing, young Lady…nothing was found," the officer explained as he closed down the machine and walked her to the door. "I'm sorry we can't be of any more help."

What did happen to Ruby's body? Abby wondered as she thanked the officer and headed for her car. She needed to find the answer to that question almost as much as she needed to find answers to help her adjust to her "birth" as a clone.

Dr. Minolo entered the farmhouse and immediately knew it was the only place he felt truly at home. His apartment in the city was just an apartment. *This place* he thought happily *has so much more!*

The woman watched him as he hung up his jacket and settled in the large blue leather armchair he had purchased for the house. "I'm glad you came," she said softly, "I was lonely today. I keep thinking there's something special I'm missing, but I can't remember what it was. Do you have any idea, Doctor?"

"You know I'd like you to call me Luis. It would mean a lot to me."

Again her eyes searched him. She knew him. She had known him for a long time. He arranged for her to live here and care for his aged mother years ago. He gave her money and showed her how to tend for his mother, Emma, who had become her close friend during the five years they had together before Emma's death.

But something bothered her…whenever she asked him questions about what happened to her, who she really was and where she came from, he never told her. He always walked around the answers and she had to accept it because he had been so kind to her. She knew the local farmer's wives gossiped about her and considered her strange, and she wondered if *they* knew who she was.

The doctor called her Matushka, which in Nortovian meant 'dear one.' *It's a pretty name, but it's not a real name, so it doesn't help me remember anything. I have such a strange longing in my heart for something that seems I can never have. What is it? Why can't I remember?*

She had remembered something, though. It came back to her now as she was looking at the doctor. When her mind reached back in search of her previous life, there were times she remembered a child…a beautiful child.

I must have loved her or I wouldn't think of her so often. Who is this child and why won't the doctor help me to remember all the things I should remember. I'm smart. He taught me to express myself better over the years, and I can even speak some Nortovian.

Dr. Minolo watched her and realized she was struggling to remember. She was in a dispirited mood lately and at times that mood continued during his entire visit. His conscience had been bothering him the last few months as well. He could be working with her to help her come out of her amnesia but instead he chose to keep things status quo where it was comfortable and he could still be with her. Things would have to change though if he was to live with himself. He could see she was suffering and it was causing him suffering as well.

"Luis, thank you for coming today. Did you bring anything this time," she asked hopefully.

He shook his head sadly. "No, I'm sorry I didn't, but perhaps I could take you to that quaint Italian restaurant for dinner. We'd be all alone there in the corner room. Would that be comfortable for you?"

The woman nodded, glancing down at her worn clothes. "What should I wear?"

"You pick out whatever you like. You always look beautiful to me." But the moment he said the words, he knew he had said too much.

She looked at him with a strange, almost fearful look.

"No...I-I changed my mind. I don't want to go to the restaurant. I don't like riding in the car. You go. I'll go another time."

She sat on a straight-backed chair across from him, and he knew that would be the end of a pleasant evening. His heart ached. He wanted so much to hold her close. All these years he had grown to love her more than he could have ever imagined, but he could never show his love. Now, he feared he had inadvertently exposed his emotions and she wasn't taking it well. Since he had made the remark about her beauty, he could tell she had pulled away from him emotionally and if he said more she would probably distance herself for good.

"My dear," he steered the conversation in another direction, "please come sit here and let's talk about your memory. After all the years you're been here you finally seem to be remembering some details of the past. Maybe it's time we work together to see if you can remember more important areas of your life. Should we try?"

She didn't move. She looked at him almost as if he was a stranger. "Tell me, Dr. Min…ah…Luis, you've known me all these years, haven't you? How did we meet? I never thought about it before, but you must have known me. You wouldn't have brought me here to take care of your mother if I was a complete stranger. Please, please tell me what you know about me! I have to know!"

The doctor was completely taken aback. He had no idea she was having thoughts like this and he wasn't sure just what to do about it. He wanted to help her, but could he stand to lose her? He decided to start out cautiously and just give her a few details. He spoke her given name clearly for her to understand and then continued, "I met you when you visited Nortovia years ago. There was an accident in which you were shot and hit your head when you fell. That injury to your brain was complicated by the gunshot wound, causing a dysfunction in your nervous system. That situation forced the part of the brain that houses the memory to shut down."

She was becoming agitated as if she wanted answers to everything all at once. And, although she didn't tell him, that part of her brain he spoke of *was* beginning to remember things. The things that came into her memory didn't fit together for her yet, but she desperately hoped the puzzle pieces would soon mesh.

"Why was I in Nortovia, Luis?" She looked at him with such pleading eyes that he was unable to think of an evasive answer.

"You were here with a group of people to have some medical findings announced."

"So, you must know *everything*...all about those people I was with, what it was they were going to announce and, my heavens…maybe even *why* I was shot?"

The doctor was losing control of the conversation and knew if he didn't somehow end it, he would have to tell her everything. Of course, there would be the possibility that she wouldn't remember, but what if she did? And sadly, if she didn't, he would still feel the pangs of selfish guilt for not helping her to remember. It was a lose/lose situation for him.

"Do you trust me?" he questioned, and she immediately looked into his eyes and nodded. "Then trust me to help you the way I feel is right. I don't think it would be good for you to remember things too quickly."

The woman sat listening with tears in her eyes and hands clasped tightly on her lap. "But please tell me why I keep thinking of a beautiful child. Did I ever have a child?"

He looked at her with love, but could not tell her of the visit he had had that afternoon. He could answer that question for her, but what would it do to her…and more importantly, what would it do to her feelings about him. With that in mind, all he answered was, "I don't know, Matushka."

Chapter Twenty-five

Stephen and Josh talked for hours on the patio as a warm fire blazed in Stephen's portable firebox. The coffee was gone and yet the conversation continued...still mostly one-sided, with Stephen tearfully relaying happier times, coupled with outbursts of anger and periods of doubt.

When Stephen finished his tale of misery, Josh spoke. "Stephen, I remember how strong you were when we were imprisoned in that warehouse. You seemed to be able to make everything OK for me. I looked up to you as the authority in all things. I still look up to you, but I wish you had the stability you had then. Your heart is too exposed."

The response was the same as it had been for the last several years, "Josh, don't lecture me on religion. You know how I feel about that."

Josh bent forward in his chair to look his brother directly in the eyes. "Stephen, I think you don't want a lecture because you're fully aware that what I say is true. You just don't want to admit it to yourself, or anyone else. You need God and you refuse to accept that fact and do anything about it."

Now that Stephen had had the opportunity to talk his feelings out, he was ready to discontinue any meaningful conversation. It was uncomfortable to talk about God. He had drifted away from God and figured it was too much work to get back into a meaningful relationship with him. He wasn't sure he even wanted to. Lately he had been in charge of himself. And now this problem before him...what could God do anyway? He had handled things himself for years, and he would handle this current trauma in his life. He didn't need God.

"What're you thinking, Stephen?" Josh asked after his brother's long silence.

"Well, I didn't want to get into this tonight of all nights, but you might as well know that once I face this, I'll be confident in myself to handle it. I don't appreciate your preaching that we need to rely on God to give us direction for every problem. I really don't feel I need his direction…doesn't mean I don't believe that he exists because I do. I guess I just feel he gave me a mind to make my decisions for myself."

Josh wasn't about to give up on his brother. "Think about this, Stephen. If you got a speed bike for the boys and figured you didn't need the instruction sheet. You thought you could assemble it by yourself. Well, what if you spent hours working on it and just couldn't get the bike together at all, wouldn't you finally refer to the instruction manual to get the correct directions for putting it together?"

Stephen nodded slightly as Josh continued, "When God is able to help us, and help us in the best possible way, why would we turn him down and think our way was better than his? Doesn't make sense, does it?"

Before Stephen could respond, two eight-year-olds came in and ran to their Uncle Josh for hugs. "Hey, we didn't know you were coming, Uncle Josh. Are you going to stay a few days so we can do some fun stuff?"

As Josh prepared to answer his rambunctious nephews, he looked over at his brother and saw the old "saved by the bell" look. Stephen lovingly chided them, "Hey boys, it's very late. What're you doing up?" Then turning to Josh he added, "We'll have to continue our discussion another time."

Jeremy spoke first as he usually did, "We heard your story about putting a bike together without the directions and how we need the instruction book, Uncle Josh. Kinda cool. We talk about that stuff in Sunday School."

Jason nodded his affirmation and chimed in, "Yah, and the teacher told us other stories like that. So we know about how to let God help us with stuff."

Both boys were images of their handsome father with their mother's silk blue eyes and reddish brown hair. They were identical in so many ways.

Josh knew at this point it would be useless to try to continue his conversation with Stephen, so he turned his full attention to the boys, catching up on all the details of their lives as each one tried to outtalk the other. Stephen brought out hot chocolate and a semblance of fun prevailed where sadness had been such a short time before.

By the time Abby reached her hotel room, she was despondent. She dropped her purse and jacket on the floor, shut the door and headed straight for the comfortable bed. She had to sleep…sleep. She couldn't face anything more…sleep, and the bed promised to gently help her. She climbed into it, wrapped the down comforter around her and curled up in a fetal position. However, when sleep overtook her, it wasn't a relaxing sleep of peace, it was the sleep of a worn out, emotional woman unable to cope with her circumstances.

The night drifted slowly along until the sun rose with the ensuing traffic sounds signaling the beginning of a work day. Abby arose, grabbed her robe and turned on the small coffee pot that would help her start her day. As she stretched, she was bombarded with feelings of discouragement and helplessness.

Why should I stay in this country? My main thought in coming was to find something of my identity, and then to discover what happened to Ruby. Well, now I know. There is no future here.

She called the main desk and asked the concierge to get a reservation on a flight back to the States within the next twenty-four hours. *Why stay? Why?*

Within the hour she had the flight reservation and began to get her things together. She would leave the next day at 7:00 in the evening. That done, she took a few minutes to have more coffee and some quiet time with God.

She rearranged her belongings in her suitcase and emptied her purse on the table to reorganize it. *Passport, money, makeup*...and as happened before, between her dollar bills was the crumpled list of names she had gotten from Uncle Don. As she perused it, the name listed under Dr. Minolo was Pastor Peter Petrov of the Great Redeemer Church in Zenova. She almost threw the note in the waste basket until a thought occurred to her. *Maybe the pastor will be able to answer some of the questions I have about my life in God, and he might talk to me about mom. That would lift my spirits. OK, I'll do it.*

She found the number in the directory and called wondering what he would think when he discovered who she was. After setting up an appointment for the next morning through the church secretary, she figured she'd have everything ready to go afterwards and could easily get to the airport after her meeting.

Chapter Twenty-six

The church still looked as Abby's mother had described it to Sarah. The warmth and the peaceful ambiance was a calming effect for Abby as she walked into the large vestibule. Before she had time to search for the pastor's office, a pleasant-looking man of about fifty approached her with his hand extended.

"You're the young lady who called for an appointment? So glad to have a visitor from the United States. I'm Pastor Petrov. To what do I owe this pleasure?" The pastor, whose boyish appearance was betrayed only by the grey at his temples, had a manner that instantly put Abby at ease. He was a handsome man, but what struck Abby the most were his eyes…they radiated genuine interest and concern. She instantly surmised he was a most compassionate man.

"I see you speak fluent English," Abby said as they walked to his office.

"Yes," he replied jovially, "Nortovia is becoming quite 'Americanized' as you've probably noticed when you speak to people here. They've no doubt answered you in English, right?"

"Yes, most people have, and I was happy to know that. I didn't realize English was becoming such a universal language."

By the time they reached his office she was relaxed. He motioned for her to have a seat and as she sat, she realized painfully that her mother may have sat in the same place talking to this pastor years ago. That thought almost brought her to tears, but she held them back. This was no time to cry.

She put her purse on the floor and began to carefully remove the cross necklace from around her neck. It was the special necklace the pastor had given her mother twenty years earlier as a token of love from those at the church who knew her so briefly. Her mother had given the necklace to Abby on her sixteenth birthday and told her only that she received it from a pastor when she became a Christian. Sarah had filled in the rest.

Abby laid the necklace on his desk and he looked at her quizzically. As he picked it up, he noted the metal behind the cross on which John 3:16 was inscribed: "For God so loved the world, that he gave his only begotten Son, that whosoever believeth in him should not perish, but have everlasting life."

"Oh my Dear, where did you get this?" The pastor's face was one of deep concern as he questioned her. "This was given to a dear Christian woman years ago, how do you manage to have it?"

Abby wasn't able to hold back the tears any longer as she said between gasps, "That woman was my mother, Dorcas Demitt."

"Your mother? You are little Abigail? You're that beautiful little girl who was here with Dorcas who captivated all our hearts?" As he spoke the words, he quickly came around his desk to lift her chin and look squarely in her eyes. "Oh Abigail. It is you. What a lovely young woman you are. I'm sure your mother is very proud of you. How is she?"

"My mother died a year ago, Pastor. Both she and my father were in an accident and were killed. It's been a terribly difficult time for our family." The recent grief was evident in her eyes and as she looked up at the pastor, she noticed he brushed away a tear.

"My Dear," he touched her shoulder fondly, "I am so disheartened to hear that news. They were still young, weren't they? As a pastor of course I believe that God wanted them for reasons only he knew, but as someone who was fond of your mother, I can understand the deep loss you must all feel."

"Thank you from my heart, Pastor."

"I heard from your mother several months after she had returned to the States. She told me the exciting news about your father and brothers escape from their imprisonment in that warehouse. She was so happy to find out that both of your brothers and your father had come to believe in Jesus as their Savior. What an inspiring end to their horrible nightmare."

As Abby dabbed the tears from her eyes, she searched the pastor's face and continued, "I don't know how much my mother told you of my history before they adopted me …"

Pastor Petrov looked uncomfortable. "She told me what I am sure was the whole story of the trauma you were all going through." He desperately hoped she would tell him before he had to reveal anything her mother had told him in confidence.

"Then you probably know I'm a…*clone* …?" Abby was surprised that she was able to repeat that horrible word to a stranger, but somehow this man sitting across from her radiated such godly love that she felt safe.

"Yes, Abigail. Your mother told me about it. She was so grieved for you and for what you might have to go through as you grew older. When did she tell you?"

Much to the pastor's surprise, Abby answered ruefully, "She never did." Then realizing how harsh she sounded, she finished her sentence more respectfully. "She died with the secret, but my surrogate grandmother knew the entire story and she revealed it to me just a short time ago. She even had the infamous doctor's file that verified everything. I can't even begin to tell you how devastating that was. I thought I would die. In fact my brother did have to take me to the hospital until I could become rational again."

The pastor's thoughts focused momentarily on the desperate mother twenty years earlier sobbing so hard she could hardly speak, telling him of her beloved child's identity. He shook his head subconsciously as if to get rid of the thoughts, but it didn't work because that child was now sitting right before him.

"Abigail, why are you here in Nortovia?"

Abby explained in detail the reasons for her coming, and as the pastor watched her intently he was amazed to recall her mother with the same earnestness and desperation. *What things we have to bear in this life!*

Her explanation culminated with her desperation knowing that she was a human clone. "I think the absolute worst thing about this *cloning* is that I feel I have no identity. I don't know if I'm a person, or just an entity…and the most awful doubts I have are those about my relationship with Jesus. If I'm not human, will Jesus still love me? Did he give his life for my salvation just as he did for the world, like that John 3:16 verse says? It's utterly devastating to feel like a freak, especially when that could put me in the position of losing my soul. And, what about heaven? These are some of the many questions I desperately need to find answers for. That's why I'm here in Nortovia."

Before she could even finish her story, Pastor Petrov held up his hand. "Stop. Stop right there. You are not a freak…whether you were cloned or born normally from a woman, you are not a freak. You have felt God's love since you were a child; that doesn't change just because you found out you were cloned instead of birthed."

Abby looked at him with tear filled eyes, "But what about heaven? Did Jesus die for me even though I'm not...*human*?"

The pastor leaned down and put an arm around her, just as he had with her mother years before when she desperately needed his help. "Abigail, listen to me. I'm convinced that God has made heaven accessible to *anyone* who believes in Jesus. He suffered, died and rose again for that very purpose.

"If you believe in Jesus as your Savior, you are a child of God no matter what your biological history might be. The most reassuring thing I can tell you is that God is the author of life. Life itself only comes from God and is perpetuated only by God. He offers his mercy and grace wherever that life comes from and under whatever circumstances."

"I want to believe that," Abby cried. "But did God have anything to do with my being formed even though it wasn't a natural formation?"

He paused and continued, "Have you ever heard the analogy of the potter forming a vase out of clay?" Abby looked puzzled. "Well, think of it this way: when God forms a person, he molds each and every person just as he plans. We are only the vessel that is being formed, and as such, how can we question the potter? You exist, don't you, Abigail? Well, if you exist, God has had a hand in your formation in whatever way he sees fit, even though it isn't the way he designed it to be. We don't need to question, we just need to trust him."

"I do trust him," responded Abby. "But I have trouble believing I have any identity."

Pastor Petrov lifted her hand and held it as he explained, "I want you to think carefully, Abigail. You agreed that you truly believe that Jesus died on the cross two-thousand years ago and that by doing so, he blotted out all your sins before God." Abby nodded enthusiastically. "Then if you believe that, *you* have an identity. You have identity as a person, but more importantly, you have identity in Jesus Christ.

"There's the verse in 2nd Corinthians that says, 'Therefore if any man be in Christ, he is a new creature; old things are passed away; behold, all things are become new.' *You* became a new creature when you believed in Christ…a new creature, Abigail. Remember that."

Abby was so overwhelmed with what the pastor was telling her that for a moment she sobbed uncontrollably. As she regained her composure she instantly replied, "Yes, I understand now. You have lightened the terrible shadow that has followed me. Thank you! Thank you!"

Although the shadow hadn't completely disappeared, she knew that the most painful questions had been reasoned out through God's Spirit, and she and the pastor clasped hands in true thankfulness. Much of her great burden had been lifted.

Abby wiped her eyes and sat back more comfortably in the chair thinking about all the assurances the pastor had given her. "I'm so grateful…so thankful I came here today." After relaxing in her new found joy and peace, she suddenly remembered. "With all this wonderful conversation, I almost forgot to finish my story."

"Yes, please go ahead. It'll be easier to handle now, won't it?"

Abby began once again, finishing with her unsuccessful efforts to find out about Ruby. "Dr. Minolo, the doctor here who worked with that Dr. Nick who cloned me, just told me that Ruby was dead. He said after she was shot and left for dead, she made it as far as some bushes outside the building where she collapsed and died. He said Duke came back later and "disposed of" the body."

The pastor looked surprised to hear the details and was about to question her further when she continued, "Ruby was a mother of sorts to me." She spoke in almost a whisper as if it was a dishonor to her dead mother to feel that way. "I understand that I look identical to Ruby as she looked then. And, I also understand from others that she truly did love me. Because I'm a part of her DNA, she was the closest person in my biological identity. Can you see why I would want to know what happened to her body? She should have some type of Christian burial."

"Yes, I can understand, Abigail, but I'm not sure just how I can help you. At the time your mother was here, she was terribly upset because you and she had to leave Ruby lying on a rug on the floor after she had been shot. She had to make sure that man, Duke, wouldn't get you and take you back to the doctor. That was the crux of the whole mess…that doctor who cloned you had to have you back in order to get the acclamation he needed."

"I understand you went back to that building at my mother's request but you didn't find Ruby or anything indicating a shooting there?"

"Yes," the pastor answered, "I went back there and didn't find anything. There was absolutely nothing in that room that would hint at what went on there, and certainly no body...but, come to think of it, your mother said Ruby's body was on a rug and when I went there, there was no body as I said…but, there was no rug either. I never thought about that until now. Your mother surmised that Duke went back to take the body after you and she found sanctuary here. I truly don't know."

The despondency on her face almost forced him to look away. Quietly she said as if it were the end of her journey, “The police didn't find anything there either.”

As the pastor sat listening, a thought came to him and he raised his hand happily. “Abigail, I just had a thought about a possible way we might find out about the details on Ruby's death.”

She looked up expectantly and sat on the edge of the chair. “What is it? I'll do anything.”

“I have a dear friend...one of my parishioners. He just retired from the police force, detective division, because of his age and a few health problems. If there would be anyone who could delve into the mystery of a missing body, he'd be the one.”

Abby's excitement was evident. “Oh could I meet him and see what he might be able to do? I have flight reservations to return to the States tonight, but I will definitely cancel them.”

Encouraged by her hopefulness, he picked up the phone and began the process that for Abby could be the end of the mystery of Ruby Cramden.

Chapter Twenty-seven

Adrian Boscovich was a rotund man with piercing eyes that seemed to find delight in every new adventure. He was balding but nursed the few white hairs growing on the top of his head as if they were prized possessions. His smile was engaging and, the word around the police station was that except for those he had arrested, he didn't have an enemy in the world.

He was fascinated with the call from his friend and pastor, Peter. Since retirement from the Force he had trouble keeping busy and just the thought of solving a mystery was invigorating.

The day after the call to the detective, Abby sat nervously in Pastor Petrov's office as they waited for Adrian Boscovich to arrive for the anticipated meeting. It had been difficult for her to be patient. It would be an important meeting, she knew.

The detective entered the room with a smile so broad that Abby smiled back instinctively. "Bosco! Good to see you," Pastor Petrov said enthusiastically shaking hands with his dear friend. "I'm so glad you could help us out. This beautiful young lady is Abigail Demitt from the States and she has quite a story to tell you."

"Adrian Boscovich at your service, my Dear," he said taking her hand in his. "I suppose we should get right to the point so I can determine just what it is I can do for you."

Once again Abby began her heartbreaking story, detail upon detail, culminating with her desire to find the body of the woman who could have been a part of her life. When she finished, it was the *why* that really shocked Bosco.

"Repeat that last sentence for me again," he asked incredulously. When he was absolutely sure that what he heard the first time was correct, he grasped her hand again and squeezed it. "My dear Abigail, I have never heard of a nightmare like the one you are going through. You can be sure I will do everything I can to get an answer to your question, and you can trust that everything will be held confidential. Now, tell me what you've done so far since arriving in Nortovia."

Abby filled him in on her visit with Dr. Minolo and some of the biological and technical facts he had given her about her formation by Dr. Nick.

"It was Dr. Minolo who told me that Ruby was dead. At first he kept telling me that he didn't know anything about what happened to her, but just as I was leaving he confessed he had been lying and finally told me the truth about her death."

Bosco was quiet for a moment as if to organize the information he was getting.

"OK, so the doc knew about Ruby's death. Who told him, and what did he think happened to the body?"

"Well, I was pretty shook up at the news, but I'm quite sure that Dr. Minolo said he had heard it from that Dr. Nick when they talked by phone. He said that after my mother and I left the building where Ruby had been shot and Duke wounded, Duke regained consciousness and followed us. At that time Ruby had just enough strength to crawl and grope her way out of the building. She was only able to make it to a patch of bushes outside where she finally collapsed and died. When Minolo questioned the doctor further he said that Duke went back to the building that night and took the body and disposed of it. 'Disposed of it' sounds so crude. That Duke had such an evil reputation, who knows what he did with it?"

"Well, that's what I hope I can find out for you, Abigail."

Then satisfied that he had gotten enough information to begin his investigation, Bosco pulled himself laboriously out of his chair, thanked them and began to leave. Just as he reached the door, he turned and smiled at the young woman who so obviously needed answers.

"Never fear, young lady. You can be sure I'll do everything I can to get you some answers, and one of the first people I talk to will be Dr. Minolo after I do some checking into his background. Maybe he knows more about what Duke did with the body than he's letting on. Try to relax a bit now. We'll meet again soon and discuss everything I've discovered to that point."

Then as a last minute thought he added, "And, please call me Bosco. I seldom answer to Mr. Boscovich." With that he smiled, saluted the pastor and left, excited to be involved in what seemed to be an extraordinary case.

Chapter Twenty-eight

David's attempts to get an answer to his cell calls to Abby were frustrating him. *In this world of extraordinary scientific discoveries I still can't get ahold of the woman I love.* He and Josh had discussed her absence a number of times, but he knew there was something Josh couldn't tell him. Had anyone else held back information from him that he needed, he would have been upset, but Josh was his friend and no matter what, he trusted him.

David had an overnight bag packed and ready just on the off chance that somehow he might hear from Abby and be able to join her. But as days passed and he received no pick up from Abby's cell, he was losing heart. The nights were the worse time for him. He had trouble sleeping, and when he did it was a disturbed sleep.

It was after one of those near sleepless nights as he watched the dawn appear that he decided one more time to try to call her. He had no idea where she was so he couldn't determine what time of day she might get his call. He just knew he had to give it a try…maybe she would answer this time.

Abby had finished her visit with Pastor Petrov after Bosco left and she was about to leave when her cell phone played Amazing Grace. She checked it and saw it was from David. The pastor looked puzzled when she ignored the call and indicated that she might want to answer it. Her eyes were tearing and she put her hand on her heart.

"It's David. I told you about him. He is the only man I've ever loved, and now I can't see him or talk to him again."

"Abigail, does he love you too?" She nodded as the tears flowed. "Then, I suggest you at least answer his call so that he can be sure you are all right."

She looked up at the pastor and down at her phone which continued to ring persistently. “Really? Do you think I should answer it?”

With Pastor Petrov’s encouragement, Abby opened her phone and for the first time in many days she answered, “This is Abby.”

David had become so used to hearing the cell ring with no answer that he almost hung up until he heard her voice. When he finally realized that she had actually answered, he was so stunned he barely knew what to say. As he recovered from his surprise, the words just wouldn’t stop. “Abby? Is it really you? I’ve been trying for days to get ahold of you. Are you all right? Where are you?”

She looked once again at the pastor for support and as he nodded she spoke to David for the first time since that awful revelation. “David. I don’t know what to say. I am all right. I’m far from you in the midst of something I need to work out. I need to think about what to say to you; but now I just can’t think. Please understand. I’d like to call you back, OK?”

David’s thoughts were jumbled. He had finally reached his precious Abby and knew she was all right. But on the other hand, she couldn’t even talk to him now. He wondered for a moment if she would really call him back; but he responded as a loved one would.

“Of course. I’ll wait for your call. I’m just so thankful that you are all right, and that you answered. Please remember Abby that I love you with all my heart, whether we are together right now or not…no matter what, I love you.”

Abby tried to stifle a sob but she was unsuccessful. “Oh, David, I love you too, no matter what. I will call you.” She closed her cell phone and continued to sob softly.

"What can I do? I don't know what to do," she looked frantically at the pastor who within such a short time had become her friend. "I can't tell my beloved David that I'm a *clone.* How could he ever understand that? I can't bear to think of how he would look at me then. I might be a freak to him. How could he love me as a *clone?"*

The pastor gazed at this young woman who had so much to live for and yet who was questioning everything about her very existence. This would take some prayer on his part and he would rely on God's guidance as he always did.

"Abigail. Let's go down to the church kitchen and have a good strong cup of coffee. That should perk us up and give us a better perspective. This office can be rather confining. What do you say?"

Coffee sounded invigorating to her and she took his hand as he helped her up from her chair. "I think it sounds good. Thank you."

As Abby and Pastor Petrov sat in the church kitchen drinking strong Nortovian coffee and talking, David closed his cell phone and instinctively yelled out a "YES" into the approaching dawn and took a sip of his hot coffee. Then grabbing his cell again, he immediately called and woke his friend who was still in New York. "Josh! You'll never believe it. I actually talked to Abby."

As David's words registered in Josh's waking mind, he jumped out of bed and said, "Thank you, Jesus!"

The exuberance of the two friends breached the miles between them and they did a high-five together in spirit. "What did she say, David?"

"Well, I didn't get much out of her. Just that she was far away and handling something she needed to take care of.

But, the great thing is that she still loves me and she said she'd call me after she had time to think. Isn't that GREAT?"

The young men continued their brief conversation and afterward Josh ran to wake up his brother with the news. It would be a good day.

In the church kitchen, Abby was surprised to feel a peace that she hadn't experienced in many days. She had developed a confidence in the pastor of the Great Redeemer Church and an appreciation for his godly advice, so she listened to him with an open mind and open heart.

He reiterated their earlier conversation when they discussed her worth to those who knew her, and especially her worth to God. "I can tell you, young lady, that I feel the same godly love for you now as I did the first day you came into my office even though I didn't know anything about you. Do you believe that?"

Abby believed his sincerity and nodded.

"Well, think about this. Although we see no justification for human cloning, it has happened and I want you to always remember that Jesus died for you whether you're a clone or not, and if you believe that, he's already planned a place in heaven for you."

Abby searched for the words, "I want to believe that...with all my heart I want to believe that. But do think it's possible for Jesus to love me as a human clone and not just a human?"

The pastor emphatically replied, "I think you know that your cloning hasn't altered my feeling about you as a sister in Christ. Certainly if I love you, try to understand that God through Jesus loves you every bit the same and more because you are his child. Knowing how you are loved, why do you think David wouldn't continue to love you just because of your background?"

She had to digest that a bit, so she took a long sip of coffee, closed her eyes and prayed silently. *Help me, Lord, to know what to do.* It was a simple prayer, but it opened the doors of heaven to reach a listening and loving God. By the time she finished her coffee she knew the pastor was right.

I believe that, so it's only fair for me to talk to David and give him the opportunity to decide for himself how he feels about me once he knows.

"God bless you, Pastor. I'm going to call him. Thank you. Thank you."

Her words were an answer to his prayer as well, and he gave her a brief hug as she dashed out of the kitchen, out of the church and back to the hotel to call David.

Chapter Twenty-nine

The eminent detective, Adrian Boscovich, enthused with his new assignment, rushed home from his meeting with Abby and the pastor and immediately entered all the data given him into his laptop. Though his age group often was computer illiterate, he had grasped the technology easily. His laptop was his closest friend and it held every detail of his entire caseload accumulated during his tenure with the police department. He wasn't sure just why he was keeping that information, but so far he had no inclination to destroy it.

"Let's see now. Column one: Abigail Demitt, a citizen of the United States, arrived in Nortovia to locate the body or person of a Ruby Cramden, also a citizen of the United States. Ms. Demitt was told by Dr. Luis Minolo that Ruby Cramden is dead and that a person named Duke who worked for a Dr. Nicholas Krebsny of the US disposed of the body. Just what "disposed of" means is anyone's guess. Note that both the person of Duke and the Doctor mentioned were killed in a warehouse fire twenty years ago.

"Abigail has ties to Pastor Petrov at Great Redeemer Church in Zenova, and as a friend of the pastor, I was called to use my investigative ability to help in the search.

"Column two: Ruby Cramden. Body missing for twenty years. Reported fatally wounded in the basement of Building 1400 on the Boulevard, Zenova, by a woman who spoke with Pastor Petrov of Great Redeemer Church, in the same city. The woman obviously knew this Ruby Cramden, however, due to confidentiality issues the pastor was not able to disclose the name of the woman who reported the body. Pastor Petrov didn't have any other details except that the woman reported seeing the body of Ruby Cramden lying on a rug in the front basement room. When the pastor went to investigate at the request of the woman, there was no body and no rug. He called the police department to report the information he had been given.

"The police report of the incident noted that they had been informed of the situation, and when they investigated they confirmed no body found. Several holes were found in the walls, but they were unable to establish if they were made from bullets as the holes appeared to be dug out with a sharp object and held no bullets. Due to the lack of evidence, the investigation was subsequently closed.

"Ruby Cramden came to Nortovia with several doctors for some experimental work in conjunction with Dr. Luis Minolo, downtown Zenova. The only other information available is that the doctors and Ms. Cramden were booked at the Savoy on the Boulevard for three nights.

"Column three: <u>Dr. Luis Minolo</u>. Abigail Demitt spoke with the doctor, who is not a medical doctor but a biological researcher. As mentioned earlier, Dr. Minolo told Abigail Demitt that Ruby Cramden was dead. He had lied to her at first saying that he had no idea what had happened to her, but then changed his story and gave her the news of Ruby's death. The subsequent details the doctor gave to Miss Demitt will be forthcoming after my interview with the doctor himself.

Miss Demitt's efforts to find out anything about where Ruby Cramden's body is buried or what happened to it have hit a dead end. As Dr. Minolo is the only real lead I have, I will get an appointment with him tomorrow, if possible."

"Next on the agenda: Find other people on Minolo's staff who might have any information. I will endeavor to make Dr. Minolo aware of the importance this information would be and that it will be in his own best interests to cooperate.

"End of first report."

Dr. Minolo hadn't been able to carry on any biological research since returning from Semsk. He had scared his love with his revealing remark about her beauty, and lately her memory had slowly been returning, leading her to expect his help. Any one of these facts was enough for concern, but all justified what he had been dreading all these years.

He was so deep in thought that he didn't hear the first two rings of his phone and his secretary had to buzz him to get his attention. He wasn't in the mood for any calls, but grudgingly picked up the receiver. "Yes, this is Dr. Minolo. You're who? You're doing what? How did you ever get my name, and what makes you think I would know anything about that?"

The doctor's hands began to shake. Some investigator was going to complicate everything. *That'll be number four of my fears,* he thought as he hung up the phone. An appointment with the detective had been set, much to his displeasure. He'd have to compose himself and think of some plausible answers to questions the detective would probably throw at him. This was definitely not a good time in his life.

David was on edge. He kept his cell phone in his pocket next to his heart so he'd be sure to hear it...when Abby called.

Then it came. He was in a meeting when his cell rang and he excused himself so quickly that his clients thought he was sick.

"Yes, Abby. I'm so glad you called. Could I come where? To Nortovia? Is that that little country bordering the

Mediterranean Sea? Well, of course I'll come. I'll head to the airport in New York today and wait there until I can get a ticket or fly stand-by. I'll call you as soon as I know my flight."

He had to fight off the tears of joy and relief. "I love you" were his parting words.

He rushed to find another lawyer in the firm to take the case he was working on and apologized to his bewildered clients. After a brief discussion, the head of the firm gave him a leave of absence for two weeks, and in minutes David was in his car heading home to pick up his packed-in-anticipation overnight bag.

By 11 o'clock that evening David was sitting in an aisle seat on a 747 heading for Nortovia. He had taken a minute before leaving to call Josh with the great news, and now his thoughts were completely occupied with Abigail.

Josh had stayed in New York for a couple days to be with his brother. They celebrated the news that Abby was all right and David was joining her.

The twins seemed to be adjusting to their mother's absence and even Stephen was coming around to the realization he would be a single father. Josh still struggled with his brother's lack of faith, but he had to admit Stephen was more willing to discuss that lately.

"Hey Brother, I'm afraid I'll have to be heading back to Vesta today. I've got a parish, you know, and a sermon to write for Sunday."

"I guess I knew you'd have to leave soon, Josh, but somehow it seemed real natural to be together these last couple days…almost like the old days."

Josh smiled, warmed by the camaraderie they had shared. "Brothers forever." Later as he left Stephen's home to return to Vesta, he had a genuine peace. “Stephen’s coming around at last,” he said out loud. “He’s coming around.”

Chapter Thirty

Dr. Minolo was clearly uncomfortable with the path the conversation was taking with Adrian Boscovich. He had answered some of the rather ambiguous questions the detective directed at him, but now the questions were getting more specific.

"So as I understand it, Dr. Minolo, you were associated with the now deceased Dr. Nick Krebsny of the US?" The doctor hesitantly nodded, and the detective continued, "Just what type of work was that, Doctor?"

"Ah...we were just working on some biological experiments...nothing of any value, certainly nothing that was earth-shattering," the doctor stuttered. "Why are you asking me all these questions? Are you interested in biological research?"

"Me? Heck no, I don't even understand it. My interest is in you personally and what you might know about the death of a woman that supposedly occurred about twenty years ago."

Hearing that, Dr. Minolo began to perspire and was visibly nervous. "Why would you come to me inquiring about a woman's death years ago? What would I have to do with anything like that?"

"Well, Doc, from what I hear you knew the woman, and frankly I don't have anyone else that I know of who did know her. The name is Ruby Cramden. Does that ring any bells for you?" As the detective spoke he carefully observed Dr. Minolo's agitation and made a mental note of it.

"I...ah...met a woman named Ruby Cramden who came to Nortovia many years ago with Dr. Krebsny, but I can't really tell you anything about her. She was quite a handsome woman as I recall."

The detective persisted. "Are you *sure* you don't know any more than that about this Ruby Cramden? The story goes that she was shot and left to die in some office building in the city…on Broadway, I believe."

"No…ah, I should say, yes I am sure I don't know any more than I told you. Dr. Nick really didn't confide in me and our work together was finished after two days, so I really can't help you." Dr. Minolo stood at his desk indicating to the detective that the conversation was over.

But, Adrian Boscovich ignored him and continued his interrogation. "Dr. Minolo, don't mess around with me. I'm no rookie. I have it on good authority that you *did know* Ruby Cramden, that you are aware that she is dead *and* that you know how her body came to disappear."

The doctor grabbed his desk and found his chair, weakly lowering himself into it. What he had feared was happening. He had to take a moment to figure out an answer to that…tell the truth, or lie again?

"Detective, I wasn't completely honest with you because I wasn't present for any of those incidents, I was only given the information from others. Yes, I did know Ruby Cramden, only slightly through Dr. Nick. I was told by the doctor that there had been a gun fight and Ruby had been shot. Somehow she had strength enough to crawl out of the building where she collapsed and died. The only other information I heard was that Duke, the doctor's bodyguard, went later and got her body, disposing of it somehow. I don't know what he did with the body, and I never asked. I just wanted to stay out of it."

"Quite a different story than you first told me, isn't it? Somehow when a person lies once, it's difficult to believe other things he says."

Dr. Minolo seemed to be calmer now that he had revealed some details of his story, and rose to physically escort the detective to the door.

"I do have another appointment, Detective, so please excuse me."

Detective Boscovich stood and walked to the door. "One last thing, doctor. Mrs. Kluski, in your anteroom is your present secretary, I assume?" To which the doctor answered affirmatively. "Has she been your secretary all these years? And would she have been with you at the time Dr. Krebsny and his group came to Nortovia?"

This was a leading question for the doctor, but one he had to answer. Mrs. Kluski would tell the detective herself if she were asked.

"Yes, Mrs. Kluski has been with me all these years, but I seriously doubt if she ever met this Ruby person or knew anything about her."

"I assume you'll have no objection to me talking with her sometime in the next few days, Doctor?"

"No objection at all," Dr. Minolo replied.

The interview was over, but not for Bosco. He wanted to talk with this biological researcher further, but needed more input first. As he made his way out of the office he checked the anteroom for Mrs. Kluski, but she was not at her desk and not in sight. Over his shoulder he called to Dr. Minolo, "Please tell Mrs. Kluski that I'd like to talk with her tomorrow and that I'll call her. Thanks."

If Adrian Boscovich had known that would be the last time he would ever see Dr. Minolo, he might have insisted the doctor answer more questions even if he didn't yet have all the facts he needed. But he couldn't foresee what would happen within the next hour on the busy thoroughfare heading out of the city toward Semsk.

The air terminal in Zenova was bustling with people speaking foreign languages of all kinds and dressed in ethnic attire from Asia, other Mediterranean countries and Europe. Nortovia was the center for connecting flights throughout the world, and because of the numerous people converging on the terminal daily; the original terminal had expanded to four additional buildings over the years.

Abby arrived as David's plane pulled up at its assigned gate. She stood excitedly next to the roped off area hoping to see him the minute he came through the door. Her anticipation matched David's as he almost ran up the ramp to the exiting door into the lobby.

He quickly surveyed the area near him and there she was. He couldn't believe his eyes, she was there waving and smiling and rushing toward the opening of the gate to get to him. In minutes they were together and time stood still. All the passersby heard was each of them repeating over and over, "I love you!"

Later, when they were alone in her hotel room and able to talk between long-awaited kisses, Abby suddenly sobered as she wondered how she would relate the horrendous news to her love.

"What is it, Abby? Are you worried about something? Can I help?" David's love for her defined her every mood and body language. "Did I do anything to cause your concern?"

Abby looked at him with tears rimming her deep blue eyes. "Oh no, David. You did nothing. It's me, and what I have to tell you."

"You mean why you're here and just what you're looking for?"

Now the tears began in earnest. "David, I don't know how to tell you. I don't know what to say. You may never understand," she wept openly.

David had thoughts of his own. "Abby, it's much too soon to talk seriously. I just got here and we have all the time in the world to discuss issues. Right now, let's order room service for a special meal, and later if you're up to it we can discuss whatever it is that's so troubling for you. How does that sound?"

Abby agreed readily, anything to avoid the inevitable discussion. "Oh yes, let's do that."

Within the hour they were enjoying delicacies native to Nortovia and thoroughly enjoying the cappuccino, and each other.

Chapter Thirty-one

The cars and trucks on the throughway outside of Zenova were speeding. Many were weaving in and out of traffic, making for hazardous driving under the best of conditions. For Luis Minolo it wasn't the best of conditions. He had just had what he considered an inquisition from a retired police detective and he was sure his credibility was in question. His only thought was getting to Semsk and the little farmhouse that gave him comfort and a reason for living.

A truck passed him and entered the lane in front of him too quickly. The doctor turned the steering wheel sharply to avoid hitting the truck, but his sports car wasn't able to correct its path and headed straight for an oncoming van.

Six cars piled up because of the head on crash and the doctor's car was at the bottom of the mangled rubble. A gasoline spill was growing rapidly on the highway and within moments the explosion occurred.

The capital city radio station broke into their regularly scheduled programming to bring the news of the devastating crash. "It is unbelievable, Ladies and Gentlemen. The death and destruction cannot be described. At this time we have learned the name of the driver of the car which first hit the van…the name is Dr. Luis Minolo, a prominent biological researcher with the City of Zenova. The doctor was dead at the scene. He had no surviving relatives. Names of other victims are pending the notification of next of kin. Stay tuned for later news on this terrible crash."

Abby wasn't aware of the news about Dr. Minolo. Her mind and heart were entwined with David and the romantic meal they were sharing.

Adrian Boscovich, however, did hear the name on his car radio and quickly set the volume up so he wouldn't miss any of the details. *Terrible news,* he thought as more and more descriptions of the crash site were given. *Poor guy...no family either. Bad news all around. Now what? Where do I go from here?*

He decided his investigation would have to take a new turn now that his main lead was gone. He'd definitely have to talk with Mrs. Kluski and learn anything he could about other associates of Dr. Minolo, but that would be difficult. She had been the doctor's secretary for years so she was probably devastated.

He decided to stop at the office the next morning on the off chance she might be there. He could offer his help. He needed to talk to her as soon as possible, so offering to help might be a better way to learn something without upsetting her more.

David and Abby had finished their meal. It had been perfect, as they enjoyed every minute of their time together. Next on their romantic agenda was to walk through the nearby park and get some fresh air. On the way they stopped by the hotel's front desk and David registered for a room not far from Abigail's.

The park walk was the culmination of the beautiful time they had shared together already. As the path curved up and down inclines, each area was resplendent with flowers of every kind and colors that stopped them in their tracks to gaze. It was an enchanting time, one Abby truly needed in her journey. David couldn't stop smiling with happiness.

As glorious as their walk in the park had been, Abby knew she couldn't put off her discussion with David any longer.

"David, could we go back to my room now? I do need to tell you about myself while I still have the courage to do so."

David continued to smile at her as he nodded graciously, but inside he wasn't smiling. He had secretly hoped and prayed that Abby just had to get away and think for awhile, but deep down he knew her news must be serious…most assuredly serious.

When they returned to the hotel, David took a moment to get his suitcase and other baggage situated in his room. While he was gone, Abby got on her knees next to her bed and prayed that God would give her the right words to explain her awful story to David, and, "please, please let David understand and still love me!"

When he returned, she took his hand and led him to the settee under the bay window overlooking the flowering park they had just experienced. She was still silently praying as she began.

In Vesta Josh was silently praying also, but he was praying for his brother. Thoughts of their childhood came and went through his mind and a few times he even chuckled out loud at some antic he remembered. They were good buddies. Josh had always looked up to his brother and thought of him as so much older and wiser, when actually Stephen was only two years older than he.

In the midst of his thoughts, the phone rang. "Stephen!" Josh yelled out loud. He was so surprised to hear from his brother at that very moment he had been thinking and praying for him.

"Josh, the boys have been bugging me to bring them to Vesta for the weekend, and get this…they want to hear you preach on Sunday. I suppose they think they'll get a front row seat," Stephen quipped out of nervousness.

"Great. That would be great. There's someone I'd like you to meet after church. I'm getting serious about her, Stephen, and I'm quite sure she feels the same way."

"Well hey, that's worth the trip alone," Stephen teased. "Can't remember when you last had a real girlfriend…about time, I'd say. We'll be there sometime in the evening on Friday. You have room to put us up, don't you?"

"You bet, brother. I'll look forward to it. See you and the boys then."

After the conversation with his brother, Josh sat down at his desk and quickly wrote an outline for what he hoped would be his "best sermon yet."

As Abby related fact after fact to David, his face mirrored absolute unbelief. He kept trying to say something in response, but she held up her hand indicating she needed to finish first. The more she told him, the more he was unable to grasp what she was saying. *It's impossible, isn't it? No one could be a real human clone, at least that's what we've heard all these years. Where would she get an idea like that?*

But as Abby gave him details, he had no choice but to believe her. He gazed at her and could see that Abby herself knew she was cloned from this…Ruby person.

When she finished, she looked directly into his eyes hoping he'd have some response, but he didn't. He was utterly without words. He opened his mouth several times and began to say something, but nothing came. It was as if he had been hit by a truck. He was in shock.

Finally, in robotic motions he rose from the settee, touched her hand and walked out of the room. The moment the door shut Abby burst into tears. She continued to cry far into the night, almost afraid to move from her spot in front of the window. She stayed in that position, finally falling into a restless sleep until the dawn began filtering through the window.

Chapter Thirty-two

"I'm so sorry for your loss, Mrs. Kluski. I realize what a shock Dr. Minolo's death must be and I don't want to add any problems for you. I just thought there might be some way I could be of help to you," Adrian Boscovich spoke softly to the woman engulfed in tears.

His hunch had been right and she was there at her desk early the next morning handling the important tasks the doctor might have wanted taken care of.

Yesterday when she ushered him into Dr. Minolo's office she was a well groomed professional secretary; but today she was a grey-haired woman whose age was obvious in the lines of her face. She was dressed in jeans and a sweat-shirt and her hand shook as she grabbed for another tissue.

"Forgive me if I can't talk sensibly today. This is the most devastating news I've ever had. He was such a good man and I loved every minute that I worked for him. I just can't seem to get organized. I'm sorry, what did you ask again?"

"I'm wondering if I can be of help."

"I don't know…I really just don't know. Could I call you if I think of something you can do? Do I have your number?"

"Yes you do. Please call anytime." Bosco began to leave, but as if on cue he turned back to the distraught woman and added, "I do hope you don't mind if I ask you a question while I'm here. It would save us both time later …"

She looked up at him as if trying to decide whether to be irritated with him or just to accommodate him. "Oh all right…just one, please."

"As we were talking I happened to wonder if the good doctor had any associates over the years that I might get in touch with so you don't have to do that painful job." Bosco even surprised himself with that clever idea.

Mrs. Kluski wiped the tears and opened her desk drawer. Pulling out a steno pad she thumbed through it, getting more impatient with every page. "Oh where is it?" She moaned at the thought of having to think of anything but the tragedy that had just taken place. "Here." She handed him the pad and busied herself sorting through the files that had accumulated over twenty years.

"Thank you. I know what an imposition this must be." He scanned the page and saw two names that might be of interest. The first name was somewhat blurred as Mrs. Kluski's tears had smeared the ink, but Bosco could make out Dante. The last name looked like Crisno. Next to that was the name Fredrico Arman. The address for them was a Zenova address.

"Mrs. Kluski, do you know if these two gentlemen are still living at this Zenova address?"

"I doubt it," was her brief and only response.

Not wanting to push it, Bosco quickly wrote down the two names and the address, then handed back the steno pad. "Please trust that I'll try my best to locate these two men so they will be aware of the doctor's death. Thank you...and don't expect to handle everything today. Try to get some rest."

She nodded absently as he left the office, once again wiping her tears as if that gesture would make things miraculously better.

Bosco almost ran to the 14th Floor elevator. Fortunately it was only a matter of minutes and he was on his way to the lobby. In his car he called his friend Peter Petrov and informed him of the chain of events that was leading him in a new direction.

"I tried to reach Abigail in her hotel room, but there was no answer. Will you call her for me, Peter, so I can continue following these new leads?"

After Bosco's call, the pastor tried several times during his busy morning to reach Abby, but to no avail. *Maybe her David arrived and they're spending the day together*, he thought as he put the matter aside and did some of his paperwork. Had he known the anguish Abby was going through, he would have done all he could to help her.

When Abby finally stood after sitting the entire night on the settee, she was so stiff she could barely move. She tried to revive herself by splashing cold water on her face, combing her hair and finally changing clothes…but nothing worked. The pain of David's rejection throbbed through her mind. She could still see the look on his face as she gave him the details of her background. *Will I ever be able to forget that look?* Her eyes felt gritty from the countless tears shed. She pulled back the covers of her comforting bed, but before she could crawl in the tears began again.

David had been awake all night as well, mulling over each word that Abby had spoken. The word *clone* kept ringing in his ears and he desperately wanted to scream it away. *I love her, what can I do? Who can even help me with this?* He stopped and fell to his knees and prayed to God who always answered his prayers. The answers he received weren't always the ones he wanted, but the prayers were always answered nevertheless, and David had the faith that whatever answer he got it would be for the best.

His prayers persisted until he realized his knees and legs were beginning to cramp up. As he rose he felt considerably better, but a thought occurred to him. *I've been thinking only of myself. What about Abby? What agony and pain she must be going through with this horrible revelation. A clone...a clone. How can she even cope with that knowledge? I can't give up on her. I love her too much...she's my very life. Somehow there's got to be a way God will help us deal with this.*

As he stood by the window, he glanced at the brightening sky and smiled. The darker clouds of dawn had given way to reveal a ray of glistening sunlight boldly pushing through the clouds. It was then David knew what he had to do.

Chapter Thirty-three

"I'm sorry, Dante Crisno died two years ago." The reply from the building superintendent was brief but definite and dampened Bosco's spirits considerably. When Bosco had approached him a few minutes earlier, he had seemed to be familiar with the name and Bosco was encouraged until the super checked his records.

Not about to give up, Bosco asked, "Do you have any information at all on an associate of Mr. Crisno named Fredrico Arman?" Bosco tapped his fingers nervously on the countertop as he waited for the superintendent to look once again through his file.

"Sorry, can't help you there either."

Bosco left the run-down apartment building and headed for the police department that had been his home while serving on the Force. Although he hated to take advantage of his position as a retired officer, he decided it was the only real break he might get in the case.

As soon as he walked into the familiar offices, he heard the usual greetings, "Hey Bosco! How're ya doin'?" The sentiments echoed through the halls as he headed for the Record's Department. "Keepin' busy, old man?" "Got a gal to take care of you yet, you old bachelor?" It was good to be back in his old surroundings again, but especially good because he knew he could leave whenever he wanted...he'd still be retired.

"Dolly, got an assignment for you," Bosco greeted his old friend. She gave him an affectionate smile and indicated she'd be happy to help. "Would you check the files and the computer records for a Fredrico Arman, A-R-M-A-N, associated with a Dr. Luis Minolo twenty years ago or so?"

"Just say the word, Sweetie. I'm on it. Go get yourself some coffee, I'll meet you in the cafeteria soon as I find anything." Dolly was one of the long-time efficient records personnel who could be counted on to find almost anyone, and who it was rumored had always had a "thing" for Bosco.

Bosco sat in the cafeteria staring out the window at the busy street wondering what his next move would be. *If there's no record of this guy, I'm out of luck for now.* He mentally went over other possible areas of information on Dr. Minolo when it occurred to him that the doctor must have had some kind of will. It would be a long shot, but certainly one he'd investigate.

In fifteen minutes Dolly walked up to his table with a note and a broad smile. "This looks like your guy, Bosco. What do you think?"

On the note was written, Fredrico C. Arman, Lab Assistant to Dr. Luis Minolo and the date was just as Bosco had said. Other jobs were listed since that time and at the bottom was an address in a small city north of Zenova in the forest area.

Bosco gave her a hug and she giggled, blowing him a kiss. His next task was to find Fredrico, one way or another.

Abby hesitantly opened the door, and seeing David her first instinct was to shut the door again. She was too ashamed to see him. Last night he hadn't even been able to look at her or to say a word after she divulged her painful secret. *Why is he even here?*

She stood at the door looking at her love with a sense of acute loss. David reached out for her, but she backed away, afraid she would be wounded again. Last night was a nightmare she had to forget.

"Abby, my dearest Abby," David whispered as she backed further into the room away from him. "Please listen to what I have to say. Would you sit down and when I'm finished, you can tell me to leave if that's what you want."

Abby sat as if waiting for something terrible to happen. She wasn't able to speak and only nodded.

David cleared his throat several times and then began. "Abby, last night you told me something that was absolutely unbelievable…something so shocking that my mind wouldn't assimilate it. I wanted to understand, but for some reason I just wasn't able to grasp it."

Abby was sitting upright, shoulders back, hands clasped tightly in her lap and once again the familiar tears drifted down the worn paths on her cheeks. It was as if she was waiting for the firing squad to shoot.

"I think I was in shock after you told me. I couldn't speak. All I could do was go to my room where I could think." He walked slowly toward her and as he reached her side, he dropped to his knees and buried his head in her lap.

"Please forgive me for walking out. I never want to hurt you. You must have suffered enough already. I only want to be with you and to help you through this, not to make things worse for you."

Abby was filled with a myriad of emotions from surprise, to relief, to a gentle peace and finally to a deep overwhelming love for the man who so obviously was sharing her pain. She touched his face and gently said his name. He looked up at his love and saw her smiling. "Do you still love me, Abby? Even after I walked out last night?"

She didn't answer him, just reached over to help him up and put her arms around him in a hug that unequivocally answered his question.

The embrace sealed their devotion to each other and wiped away any questions. "Abby, I need you to know that I love you no matter what. You are perfect to me and have been since I first saw you. You have a good mind, a fantastic disposition and you are a woman of great faith. Along with all this, I might add you are breathtakingly gorgeous. I don't *care* if you're a human or a human clone. It doesn't change my love for you and it never will."

Abby grabbed David's hand and squeezed it so hard he had to flinch. "I love you with all my heart too, David. Your understanding means more to me than almost anything in the world. Thank you."

"You know, don't you, that God loves you just the same? Human cloning most likely wasn't what God intended when he formed man and woman, but you believe in him. That makes you his child as much as I am. Do you believe that?"

"Yes, I'm beginning to, David. I talked with a wonderful pastor here. He's the pastor my mother saw twenty years ago and the Holy Spirit used him to help my mother believe in Jesus."

David looked puzzled, and Abby grabbed him by the hand. "Let's go for a walk in our park. It's such a spectacular day, and I have so much more to tell you."

Chapter Thirty-four

The city of Dormsk was just waking when Adrian Boscovich drove down the main street. He had to take special care not to get in the way of the numerous bicyclists beginning their early morning routes to work. The inviting smell of fresh bread filtered through his open window and he decided to stop and try some of the local pastry before heading on to the city offices.

Once warmed by the samples of fresh cranberry bread and a fruit-filled bagel, he began his task to locate Fredrico Arman.

In Semsk, the woman walked sadly from the market to her farm home. She was carrying a two-day old newspaper on which Luis Minolo's picture was featured. She read just enough to know that her friend was dead, and she couldn't bear to read any more of the details until she was safe in her cottage.

As she walked the distance from town, her thoughts were of the doctor. When he had taken care of her injuries, he graciously had given her shelter in the cozy cottage outside the sleepy village of Semsk, and the only thing he asked of her was to care for his invalid mother who lived there.

She smiled as she remembered the old lady who had become a dear friend over the five years she had cared for her. Emma had taught her how to knit and sew, and on her good days they would go out into the garden where she displayed her special gardening expertise.

The doctor came often to visit them both and she considered him a friend as well. She had wondered from time to time if he had more feelings for her than friendship, but because she didn't share those feelings, she never thought much about it. What would happen now? Could she still continue to live in the cottage that had been her home for so long?

As she continued walking, something began happening. The shock of reading the horrible news of her friend's death seemed to be triggering thoughts that were new to her; thoughts that brought people's faces and places into her mind. The faces had only been slight recollections before, but now were slowly taking on identities she seemed to know. Even some of the places seemed to be more detailed.

And then, it appeared once again…the face of the beautiful child she thought of so often. "What does this mean?" she cried out to the deserted road. Her cry seemed to echo off the surrounding countryside.

By the time she was safely seated in her comfortable rocking chair, the thoughts were distressing her. *If only Luis could be here to tell me what they mean…but I'll never see him again.* The tears flowed down her worn but still attractive face as she opened the paper to read the short detailed account which meant the end of the friendship that had enabled her to go on all these years.

"Car accident on the throughway…biological research career…remains cremated immediately…no memorial service…no family." That was it, just a paragraph for her friend. She put the paper on the table and leaned back in her rocker thinking of the times she and the doctor shared. Her tears mingled with smiles at many of those memories and then, she sat up with a start.

It's good to remember the nice times I had with Luis…but I'm starting to remember happenings from long ago as well. Sometimes I'm afraid of what I'll learn if all those things return. Do I really want to bring back all those memories?

The bright sun that had earlier shone through the windows of the cottage was changing into the darkening shadows of evening, and all the while the woman sat slowly remembering bits and pieces of a life she had completely forgotten. She hadn't moved. She hadn't eaten. She had been engulfed with sorrow over the death of her friend and now fear at the awakening memories creeping steadily into her mind.

Soon the sun had completely disappeared. Night had come, and the memories were beginning to fit together.

Chapter Thirty-five

Mrs. Kluski instinctively returned to the office at 8:00 each morning. She wasn't sure just why she felt the need to do that, but until she was forced to leave, she would continue to be there.

Today her project was to go through the safe Dr. Minolo kept in his office. He had shared the combination with her, but he trusted her implicitly and never expected her to use it except in an emergency. She had been assured there was nothing of interest in the safe but a few pamphlets and reports on biological findings.

Slowly and gently she turned the knob to each precise number until the old safe door creaked open. *Not much in here.* She pulled out several papers and an envelope. Then she noticed a black box almost hidden in the back of the safe. Gathering all the documents and the box, she spread them out on the work table near her desk and gently closed the door of the safe as if to say good-bye once again to memories.

She sifted through the papers, discarding most of them, except the sealed envelope. She hesitated for a moment before opening it as it was from the legal firm the doctor hired years ago, but now she felt it was her responsibility to go through everything in the safe.

The envelope contained only two sheets of paper. The first one was the doctor's original Last Will and Testament leaving all his earthly goods to his mother, Emma Doral Minolo. Mrs. Kluski liked Emma. The woman was an invalid who had been enjoying personalized care at a nursing facility until her son's failed project with Dr. Nick Krebsny.

"Poor, Dr. Minolo," Mrs. Kluski sighed, "he lost everything, and it took years to get established again. He even had to take his mother out of the facility and settle her in her old country farmhouse in Semsk. Good thing he got some woman to live there and take care of his mother for those years until she died."

The second paper had fallen to the floor and as Mrs. Kluski reached for it she realized it was another Will dated after the original one. She glanced around the room as if she were doing something illegal and then read the brief words on the page.

"What? I don't believe it," Mrs. Kluski spoke to the empty room, "he left his entire estate and all his earthly goods to a…Ruby Cramden." *Who in the world is Ruby Cramden?*

As the question echoed in her mind, the mysterious black box summoned her attention. On the outside was a note in Dr. Minolo's handwriting stating that on his death, the box was to be given to the law firm handling his Will and they would see to it the contents would be returned to the owner along with the inheritance when the numerous legalities were completed.

Mrs. Kluski put the Wills on the desk and pried open the box. She was appalled at the contents. Inside she found a handgun and a passport belonging to this person…Ruby Cramden, the same woman who was going to get the entire inheritance.

What in the world does this mean? Should I report this to someone, or just give it to the lawyer as the instructions say?

Within the hour she had answered her own question, put the papers back in the envelope and resealed it, grabbed the black box and was on her way out the door to hand deliver the doctor's last important papers to the lawyer's office.

If I was being truly honest, she thought, *I had hoped the doctor might leave me at least a share of his estate. I've been a faithful secretary all these years.* But her thoughts were of no avail.

Stephen and the twins walked up the flower-lined path leading to the door of Josh's church. The day was sparkling and crisp, and the boys were chattering away excited to hear their uncle give a sermon. Stephen was less excited, but happy to have a diversion from his pain over Tiffany, and his worry about Abby. It was always a treat to visit Josh. He seemed to know just what eight-year-old boys like to do for fun, and Stephen remembered Josh also made the best cappuccino.

The Community Christian Church had been built about five years previous and the furnishings were planned to be sturdy and tastefully plain. But, the cross…that was the main focus at the altar and to all who saw it. It was awesome. One of the parishioners had spent months delicately carving it out of cherry wood and polishing it to a mirrored shine. Even the twins noticed and pointed so their dad could take note.

Josh saw them immediately as he opened the service and smiled broadly. *Please let my sermon touch hearts this morning, especially my brother Stephen's.* The hymns were sung and Josh could hear his nephew's enthusiastic singing over the rest. When it was time for the sermon, Josh began slowly with prayers surrounding every thought.

"Why are you all here today?" he asked to the surprise of the congregation. "I'm very glad you are, but I'm also curious as to just *why.* Some of you may be here out of habit or maybe you feel guilty if you don't attend, others may be here because you want to make an impression on someone; still, I hope most of you want to hear God's Word and to worship him."

Stephen looked around at some of the other people present and was surprised to see many smiling and nodding.

"Let me remind you," Josh went on, "that we are not alone here. The Holy Spirit of God is present with us, touching hearts, opening understandings and helping us to see our sin. Oh…does the word 'sin' make you feel uncomfortable? Just remember, we're all full of it…sin, that is, and God the Father can't stand sin. On our own we can't get rid of the evil that's in us, so what do we do?" Looking around, Josh continued. "Well, God had a plan. Anyone know what that was?"

Fifteen little hands went up throughout the congregation and the children all yelled somewhat in unison, "God sent Jesus!" Stephen and the twins were astonished at the happy response of the little ones and Jason poked his brother, "Hey that's cool."

Josh continued, "God did send his Son, Jesus, and his task was the most difficult one anyone would ever have to do. He willingly let people make fun of him, put a crown of thorns on his head that caused blood to flow down his face, and willingly took the bloody beatings the Roman soldiers enjoyed inflicting on him. You know *why* he did this, don't you?"

At this question, the congregation clapped enthusiastically and Josh went on, "He suffered through that and then had to endure the excruciating pain of being nailed to a wooden cross. But while he was hanging on the cross, the most extraordinary thing happened…through his suffering, bleeding and then death, he offered his earthly life as payment for all *our* sins."

Another round of applause and this time a few cheers were heard. Stephen and his sons were feeling the love and the spirit in that church and were inspired to clap with the group. "You remember I just mentioned God hates sin? He can't even be present where sin is present. So, because of the gift Jesus gave by his suffering, death and resurrection, all *our* sin is wiped clean...and now we are children of God the Father.

"I'd say that's the greatest news we've ever heard, and I'd say that our Salvation is the greatest gift ever given. And what do we have to pay to receive this gift?" Suddenly a little three-year-old girl stood up proudly and yelled, "Nothing!"

The place broke up in laughter and when it quieted down Josh said, "Yes, Jennie, you gave the right answer. Jesus' gift is free. All we need to do is just believe it!"

Something was stirring in Stephen. He had heard the words before and even believed them, but he lost the personal relevance. Now, the assuring words of Salvation were tugging at his heart. As he watched his sons clap and cheer, and then looked at his brother speaking the words of God, the Spirit present among them touched Stephen. The faith he had known as a child was returning and he felt like a new man. He was so moved that he didn't even hear the rest of his brother's sermon.

As Stephen loudly added his Amen to the chorus of those in the church, Josh had to stifle a few tears as he watched his brother come back to God.

Chapter Thirty-six

"David," Abby said expectantly, "I want you to go with me to meet Pastor Petrov. He's been such a help."

David smiled. "He has quite a history with your family, doesn't he? Of course I'd like to meet him."

"And, you'll love him. He's so kind and explains things so well. He is even the one who called his friend Adrian Boscovich to investigate the whereabouts of Ruby's body and what had happened to her."

"I understand Ruby is an important part of your identity, Abby, but do you think you'll ever find out what happened so long ago? Wouldn't it almost be better to forget your search for answers? What if it ends in more pain and sadness for you?"

Abby was surprised to hear David say such a thing. "Don't you think that because she is such an important piece in this puzzle of my life, I *have* to find out about her? I hate to admit it, but I am already expecting the worst and would like nothing more than to leave right now with you, David, but *I can't...I just can't."*

They sat on the settee overlooking the park, each deep in thought until Abby broke the silence. "Let's not think any more about Ruby right now, David. Let's go to the church so you can meet Pastor Petrov, and then maybe we can stop somewhere for a gelato. I hear they're almost as tasty here as in Italy. How does that sound to you?"

David knew at that moment she could talk him into most anything and smiled as he watched her on the phone arranging a meeting with the pastor.

"You'd like us to meet you for lunch, Pastor?" She glanced quickly at David for his approval, and of course he agreed. "Yes, we'll be happy to meet you there."

David and Abby knew the minute they pulled up to the LaPalotte Restaurant it would be a glamorous luncheon. The parking attendant came to whisk their car away and the doorman pontifically opened the large ornate door into the elegant restaurant.

The waiter had been expecting them and graciously led them to the pastor's table. As they approached, he rose to give Abby an exuberant hug while grabbing David's hand pumping it enthusiastically. "What a great day for a get-together, and what a blessing to have you two here with me. We have much to celebrate, right?"

David nodded, smiled and looked at Abby who despite all she had been through was beaming with love. "Yes, we do," David replied genuinely touched, "and from what I understand we owe a lot of our happiness and our reunion to you. Thank you, Sir, most sincerely."

As the men engaged in conversation, Abby looked around the splendor of the room. The thick velvet drapes complimented the ornate gold and red fabric wallpaper, and the spun rayon cloths on each table tastefully displayed the delicate gold-edged silverware. Abby's eyes glistened as she gazed at the elegance, turning her head to watch David with the joy of love that almost took her breath away. Just for a fleeting moment it seemed she might be in heaven.

Adrian Boscovich was not happy. He had checked out two apartment buildings by mid-morning and still had not located Fredrico Arman. He was losing patience as he lumbered up the cement walk to the third apartment on his list. The building was white stone and well kept. Even the security seemed top-notch. The last names were not listed under the phone in the entryway, but as Bosco scanned each name thoroughly, he was relieved to see "Fredrico" listed on one of the bottom boxes. He pushed the buzzer several times impatiently and to his relief a voice answered.

"Fredrico here. What can I do for you?"

Bosco cleared his throat so he could speak distinctly into the miniscule speaker, "I'm from the police department in Zenova and I'd like very much to talk with you a few minutes," he lied just a bit. "Shouldn't take long. May I come in?"

The pause from the speaker seemed interminably long, but finally the voice answered in the affirmative and the door buzzed for his entrance.

The apartment number indicated the lower level and Bosco hurried to get there before Fredrico might think about the visit and change his mind. "102, 103…ah, here it is, 104." The door opened before Bosco could even knock and a man in a wheel chair was ushering him into the room.

"I'm Fredrico Arman, and you're …?"

Bosco leaned over and shook Fredrico's hand, "I'm Adrian Boscovich, *formerly* with the Zenova Police Department. I apologize for misleading you, but I'm doing some private detective work now and I was afraid you might not see me. I'm representing a young woman who is trying to locate someone, and as a former employee of Dr. Luis Minolo, I thought you might be able to help."

"Oh, the doc. Sure, I worked for him, but when his project failed about twenty years ago, Dante and I took off. I'm sorry we left the guy…what do the American's say, 'out on a limb,' but there was no future there for us after that."

Bosco acknowledged the phrase and carefully told Fredrico the news of Dr. Minolo's death. "I didn't know if you'd heard about it."

Fredrico's face drooped and Bosco thought he saw a few tears forming in his eyes. "I hadn't heard. What a shame. He was a good biologist, just got mixed up with the wrong people back then. How'd he die?"

"Car accident on the throughway going toward Semsk. Quite a pile-up and several people besides the doctor were killed as well." After waiting a respectable amount of time, Bosco continued, "If you don't mind my asking, how did you come to be in a wheelchair?"

Fredrico sighed and turned quickly, wheeling himself into his airy kitchen. "Come have some coffee…Adrian, is it?" Bosco nodded patiently waiting for the answer to his question. "It was just after Dante and I took that woman's body out of that building on the Boulevard. I twisted wrong and messed myself up good. Then, had the bad luck to go to a doctor whose questionable surgery made it worse, so I've been in this chair for close to twenty years."

Bosco could hardly believe his ears. *Did he say he and Dante took a woman's body twenty years ago?* "I'm sorry, I didn't know about your injury. How did you happen to be moving a woman's body anyway?" Bosco was trying to keep his questions low key even though he knew this was his first real breakthrough.

"Oh that. That American doctor Minolo was working with called and told him about a skirmish in that building, so the doc sent us over there right away. He didn't know just what had happened, but he evidently suspected someone was hurt and wanted us to check it out and bring any victims back to his office. When we got to the building we found the body of this woman, a passport and a gun, so we did what we were told, discretely of course."

By this time Bosco's interest was obvious. "Fredrico, didn't you guys find any blood or anything at the scene?"

Fredrico was beginning to feel as if he was being interrogated. "There was a lot of blood on the rug, but we just rolled her up in the rug and put her and the gun and stuff right in our van. We saw a couple bullet holes in the walls, so we dug out the bullets and scraped the holes bigger so there wouldn't be any clues."

He looked at Bosco with fear, "Hey, we didn't do nothin' illegal…just moved a body from one place to another and took care of a couple bullets. It was up to the doc to do any reporting."

"Just one more question, do you know the name of the woman? And what the building number was?"

Fredrico looked up at the detective and wondered if he had said too much and could actually be in trouble. "Ah…I don't know."

Bosco had perfected his keen observations of human behavior years ago and knew from the sudden change in Fredrico that he'd have to adjust his tactics a bit if he wanted to get all the information he needed.

"Listen. You won't get into trouble answering my questions. According to the police records twenty years ago a disturbance was reported in Building 1400 on the Boulevard, but when they checked it out, they found nothing. So you have nothing to fear as far as the police are concerned. Can you tell me, was that the building where you found the body?"

Fredrico was hesitant and clearly didn't know what to do, so Bosco quickly added, "Trust me, I just need the information to find out something about what happened to that woman, if it's the same one. Would you think again and see if you remember her name and the building number?"

Fredrico's demeanor changed. Bosco's encouragement was beginning to make him feel more at east. "That building number sounds about right, but I'm really not sure of the woman's name. The doc seemed to be interested in what happened to her, so he just took over. Dante and I left her there and went to a bar. Dr. Minolo must have disposed of the body because we never saw it again."

"One more question," Bosco said reassuringly. "Just in case you heard the doctor call the woman a name, if I run a few names by you would you indicate if any sound familiar?"

"Sure, go ahead." By this time Fredrico was thankful the visit was almost over.

Bosco began: "How about Helen, Natasha, Serena, Ruby ...?"

"Yah, that might be it...Ruby! I think that's what the doc called her...Ruby."

Bosco smiled, shook his hand and headed for the door. "Oh," he said as though he just thought of something for the first time, "Fredrico, where did Dr. Minolo live? Did he have a home or property somewhere that you know of?"

"Not sure on that one. He lived in an apartment near his office then and once I heard him mention a place his mother owned, but she was in a nursing home when Dante and I left. That's the only place I think he ever mentioned."

Exhilarated by the valuable information he had gained, Bosco shook Fredrico's hand enthusiastically and wished him well. As he left the apartment building and the town of Dormsk, he smiled a detective's smile of satisfaction. *Maybe this will be over before long for that poor young woman.*

Chapter Thirty-seven

"I was in prison! In prison? Oh, no!" Her heart was beating faster and the tears fell. The night which should have brought her restful sleep only brought her an awareness she hadn't had for twenty years, and an awareness she wasn't sure she wanted. In the three hours after midnight, the woman's memories were returning fast and furiously. She couldn't control them, and finally out of desperation she closed her eyes and just let them come.

Her father's face slowly edged its way into her mind. He was talking to her and trying to make her understand that he wasn't fit to be her father; he had done things he wasn't proud of and he didn't seem to be able to stop. He left then and she remembered painfully that she never saw him again.

She was remembering a funeral…it was her mother's. Ruby's heart had been broken then and it was breaking again as she remembered the grief. "Oh, Mom," she cried out. "I wish we could have had more time together. Could you see the miserable life I had after you died?" She wept as she remembered her mother's graying red hair pulled to the side in the cheap casket welfare had gotten for the funeral. Her hands were red and rough, but even in death her face was one of strength and determination.

She buried her face in her hands and wept for her mother, and in a strange way she wept for her father as well. It was then the other face appeared in her memory. It was a child, a young child with vivid red hair and the most fantastic blue eyes framed with emerald highlights. The child was laughing and reaching out for her. Then she turned and was showing off her pretty dress, making a curtsey as if in front of a queen.

The woman involuntarily reached for the child into the darkness, but as she drew her hand back the face of the child and the flood of memories stopped. She shook her head slowly wanting the memories to continue, yet fearful of what they might disclose after all this time.

She closed her eyes and sunk even deeper into her comfortable rocker. Maybe now that the memories stopped she could make some sense of it all, but nothing worked. There didn't seem to be a sequence to the events and people the memories were stirring within her.

Then without warning, she could see herself running with the red-haired child. A dimly lit room brought pangs of fear and she shook slightly. She remembered pulling the child behind her to protect her. *I was shot and I shot a man! Why would I do that?*

Questioning herself, she remembered there was someone crouching near her. Who was it…a pretty woman with desperate fear in her eyes, reaching for the child. Then she knew. *Dorie…Dorie, my friend.*

She squirmed in her chair. How much more of this could she take at one time? Beads of perspiration were forming on her forehead and she had difficulty breathing. *I don't know if I want to remember more. It's so…traumatic, as Luis used to say when describing problems of life.*

The doctor was there in the past and present memory…Luis Minolo was there in her heart. She could feel his tenderness as she remembered how he cared for her, bandaged her wounds, fed her and helped her learn to walk again. *Was that after the shooting? I don't remember getting to his office, I just remember how kind and gentle he was.*

Abruptly those memories morphed into the time when he brought her to this cozy home to be with his mother. *Oh, Emma, I miss you too, she* thought…*it was so long ago.*

The grief she felt over memories of lost family and friends upset her and she determined to step out of those thoughts into the present…to freshen up, to eat a little something and rest her mind and heart for awhile.

She splashed water on her face and made a sandwich, but she could not rest her mind and her heart.

Later as she tried to sleep her rest was rudely interrupted by invading memories of another doctor. She shuddered as his face materialized. Who was he? Why did she remember his face with such dread? What had he done?

Then, his face was joined by faces of an evil looking man with a ponytail and an attractive woman in a white coat. A laboratory came to mind, a warehouse…and the child. The child was there too. *The child...the laboratory...the doctor. Oh,* she cried loudly, *he cloned her. That exquisite little child was cloned!* At that moment the realization hit her like a cyclonic wind. She closed her eyes, and rubbed her forehead as if to wish it away.

So that's where I came into the picture...they used me to clone that child! Does that make her my child? Is she mine? What was her name?

Within seconds Dorie's face appeared once again…Ruby's friend, maybe her only friend in the world. Their friendship grew out of their mutual love for Abigail. *That's it. Abigail! She's Abigail! Abby, my little Abby.*

Throughout the remainder of the night most of her memories returned. She had to stifle nausea when she remembered her criminal past and the life on the streets she had lived after her mother died. She remembered with revulsion the man she thought she loved but who only used her.

The tears flowed profusely. She now knew…*I'm Ruby Cramden, #42689, Tipka Prison. What a mess I've made of my life.*

Pastor Petrov returned to his office still immersed in the opulence of the restaurant and the joy of the special young couple who had joined him. His phone's message button was blinking, beckoning to him, but he decided to sit at his desk a few minutes and bask in the memory of the enjoyable luncheon with Abby and David. The message could wait…but within minutes his curiosity got the better of him and he listened to his voice mail.

Bosco was talking so fast it was hard for the pastor to understand him. Something about finding a strong link to what happened to Ruby Cramden, and he was going to pursue it immediately. "I'll call you just as soon as I learn anything. And, Peter please pray that this might be the end of Abby's search."

Smiling, with a thankful heart the pastor did just that.

Abby and David sat amidst the elegance of the restaurant for an hour after the pastor left. Their eyes met and love was exchanged as they held hands and talked of the miracles they seemed to have experienced during David's brief time with her.

The waiter hovered over them filling their water glasses until he needed to seat other customers at their table. He finally brought over a gold tray with a delicious chocolate treat as a subtle hint. David held up his hand and asked for just a few more minutes, and as the waiter turned to attend another table, David lovingly took Abby's hand. With all the love Abby had ever hoped to see, David asked for her hand in marriage.

"Yes," she cried loudly enough for the surrounding tables to hear, "I will marry you!" Polite applause drifted from one table to another as many shared part of the moment with the young couple. *Glorious. A glorious day.*

As Stephen walked down the steps of the church with an arm around each son, he felt a peace he hadn't felt for years. They walked to his car in quiet reflection and waited for Josh and his young woman.

Josh hurriedly shook hands with the last two parishioners and smiled at Cindy who had been waiting near him. "Come with me a minute?" he said, as he led her into the back of the already empty church.

"What is it, Josh?" she asked expectantly.

"Cindy, can we begin dating exclusively? You're very special to me and I don't want to share you with anyone."

She smiled and nodded happily.

Love was in the air…in Nortovia's elegant LaPalotte Restaurant…in the back of the small church in Vesta…and a renewed love of faith being experienced by a father and his two sons waiting in the church parking lot.

Chapter Thirty-eight

Mrs. Kluski was walking through the familiar office one last time before turning it over to the landlord for the new tenants. She pulled up the window blinds and looked down fourteen floors to the street. So many years she had enjoyed that awesome view…but no more. As she was about to leave, the door opened and she faced Adrian Boscovich.

"What now, Detective? Didn't you get enough information from me before?" She did nothing to hide her impatience and began to brush past the detective, when he reached out and touched her arm.

"Mrs. Kluski, believe me I'm not here to harass you. I have just one more question for you and then you'll never have to bother with me again."

She signed deeply and leaned against the door frame, indicating that one question was all she would put up with.

"Do you know anything about some property or home that Dr. Minolo had, other than the apartment he lived in?"

"Yes," she responded as she walked through the doorway.

"Oh, come on, Mrs. Kluski. It's the last thing I need to know…would you please tell me what you know about it?"

"No!" she answered and started down the hall. Then, within a few feet, she slowed and turned back to the detective.

"I'm sorry. I'm usually not rude to people…this whole thing has just upset me so. Dr. Minolo's mother owned a little home in the country which wasn't used for years because the doctor had been paying for an expensive retirement home for her."

She dabbed at her eyes and blew her nose before continuing. "Well, when his project with that American doctor went bust, he couldn't afford to keep his mother in that retirement place, so he moved her back to her home. I think it was in Semsk. Anyway, she was there for five years before she died. As far as I know it's just been empty since."

Bosco tried to hide his growing interest and casually asked the leading question. "Oh…just one more thing. Dr. Minolo must have had someone taking care of his mother while she lived in her home. Do you know who that might have been?"

"I don't rightly know, Detective, but you could check with the lawyer at Dansel & Sons who represented Dr. Minolo. They're handling any disposition of his estate."

He grabbed for her hand and clasped it expressing genuine thanks.

"I hope you get the answers you're looking for," she said kindly as they rang for the elevator. When they reached the lobby, Mrs. Kluski wiped her eyes and slowly left the building without looking back.

Armed with his latest good news, Bosco decided not to waste time and headed for the offices of Dansel & Sons.

The law firm was located in a modern two-story building in an upscale part of Zenova. Finding the office was easy and finding the reception area easy as well, but finding just which lawyer in the firm was handling the Dr. Minolo's estate was not easy. Oh, he was quite sure the receptionist knew that information, but she kept him waiting half an hour.

Finally, Bosco had had enough and approached the desk in anger.

"Young Lady, I've been waiting half an hour! I'm no longer asking you for the lawyer's name who's handling the Minolo Estate, I'm *telling* you to give me that information. If you can't, I'll call my contact at the police department. Maybe he'll be able to persuade you."

"You want Antush Velovich. He's handling the case. I'll find out if he can see you now." Her hand was shaking noticeably as she dialed the lawyer's extension.

Bosco's threat worked, and within minutes he was ushered into the plush office of Mr. Velovich. After proper introductions, Bosco got right to the point.

"I have a client who is searching for a relative thought to be dead, and I believe Dr. Minolo was one person who could help in the investigation. Sadly, he was killed, as you well know. But, I am asking you as his legal representative to give me whatever information you might have about the current status of his mother's home in Semsk and any possible leads as to the whereabouts of the body of Ruby Cramden."

"Hold on a minute, Detective Boscovich. I don't know if I can legally disclose that information to you. Let me have your credentials once again and I'll check with Mr. Dansel personally."

Bosco handed him his official status card with the Zenova Police Department once again and waited patiently while Mr. Velovich conferred with his superior. Within minutes he was back and smiled at Bosco.

"Normally we might have legal problems releasing any information to you, even though you have connections with the police department, but the State Assembly recently passed a law giving the legal profession more leeway in this area. Because of that and the fact that Dr. Minolo had no living survivors, I can tell you that he *did* know a Ruby Cramden and that he was *still* owner of the house in Semsk at the time of his death."

Bosco was about to question the lawyer further.

"I am sorry, Mr. Boscovich, but that is all the information I can legally disclose. I do hope it will help in your investigation."

Antush Velovich rose and walked Bosco to the door. The conversation was over.

The next morning Bosco updated his computer file on Abigail Demitt and left the city for the nearby village of Semsk. On the edge of the quaint village he stopped at a petrol station. An aging, shriveled man walked slowly out of the miniature store as the detective opened his window and inquired about the location of the Doral place. The old man was suddenly rejuvenated as he replied, "Oh, bet you're here to see that lady who lives there. My wife says she's a strange one, but we fellas, well, we think she's really something!"

Lady...what do you know? Bosco smiled. "She's really a beauty, huh?"

The attendant stood as erect as he could manage at his age and replied, "You bet."

Bosco smiled and gave the old man a thumbs up and followed the directions he had received. *Could I be that lucky?*

The dirt road wound around grain fields and rushing creeks. About a mile out of the village, he turned onto a single lane road lined with rows of ferns that seem to usher him onto the property described by the attendant. It was early afternoon and the sun was warming the countryside nicely, yet the detective noted that the door to the house was closed as well as all the windows he was able to see.

Feeling somewhat apprehensive that the house might be empty, he hurriedly jumped out of his car and headed for the door. After first knocking politely, he finally began to pound the door hoping beyond hope that someone would be there.

After minutes of pounding, he gave up and walked around the back of the house. The garden was robust with vegetables of all kinds, waiting snugly in neat rows to be picked. The sidewalk had been swept and clusters of flowers bloomed around the house, as if to keep it safe.

There seemed to be no one around, so his only recourse was to leave his business card wedged in the door and hope maybe, just maybe, he'd get a call from the house's occupant.

He drove out of the short driveway and down the road to the turnoff towards the village, while his every move was being observed from behind the curtain of the quaint little house.

"I never give up," Bosco told his friend Peter. "I'm going back to Semsk tomorrow and if no one is home, I'll go back the next day. I have to follow this lead through to the end."

The pastor knew his friend and knew he was a determined man. "You know, Bosco, I'd like to go with you. I can't go tomorrow, but if you take a drive out there the day after, give me a call. I could use a brief change of scenery, and if our Ruby is really there, I'd like to talk to her as well."

Ruby had packed her bag and then unpacked it. She had no idea what to do about this strange visitor who had pounded on her door. She could leave, but if she left her little home, where would she go? Here she had her garden and her small income from the produce at the market. How would she live if she left?

As she sat watching the sunset from her lawn chair next to the garden, those questions bombarded her, the memories bombarded her and slowly the talks she and Dorie had had about God were bombarding her. At one point, she put her hands over her ears to shut out all the thoughts.

In the early morning she left for the market and when she returned, she found a second business card next to the previous one. *What's going on? Who is this person who keeps coming out here?* Those questions accompanied her to the kitchen as she readied a needed cup of tea. Sipping the tea, she realized she had no recourse other than to stay in her home and if the man returned, hide again or meet him head on. The decision, though a step in the right direction, offered her little comfort.

The following day Bosco stopped by the church. "Peter, I'm heading out to Semsk for the third time. Are you still interesting in tagging along?"

The pastor had cleared his schedule in the hope that he might be able to take a few hours break in some manner or other, and when Bosco stuck his head in the office with the offer of a drive, he was ready to go.

As the men drove through the village of Semsk the rainclouds had moved on and the countryside was awash in colors. *A delightful day,* thought the pastor, and joined Bosco in the hope that somehow this visit would prove successful for Abby.

"Bosco, I have no idea how this will all play out if we do find Ruby, but we can never dismiss God's guidance in any situation.

The last few minutes of the drive was in silence, each man engrossed in his own thoughts about Ruby Cramden and how the outcome of their visit might affect Abby and her search.

The woman was intent on her gardening and didn't hear a car or voices until suddenly two men were standing at the edge of her garden.

As the woman turned to look at them, both men were taken aback. There could be no mistake...this had to be Ruby. She wasn't dead like Dr. Minolo had said...she was very much alive. *What a turn of events,* thought Bosco. *Who would have guessed that Ruby really was alive all this time.*

As she gazed at them fearfully, the heavier of the two men spoke to her first in Nortovian and then English as he displayed a police badge. "Please...please. Don't be afraid. I'm Detective Boscovich and this is my friend, Pastor Petrov. We'd just like to speak with you a few moments."

She rose slowly from her kneeling position.

"What is it you want of me?" she asked, close to tears. "I saw you here the other day," she said nodding toward Bosco, "Am I under arrest or something?"

He smiled and responded kindly, "No, of course not. I'm a retired detective and my pastor friend and I are interested in locating a woman or someone who might know what happened to that woman. There are people anxious to get some answers."

Pastor Petrov introduced himself by way of offering his arm to the woman to ease her exit from the garden, "We would greatly appreciate it if you would speak with us."

Ruby watched them both carefully and reluctantly showed them into her house. "Just a few minutes, though, I don't like visitors very much."

The men seated themselves after she had taken refuge in her faithful rocker. Bosco was the first to speak. "I'll get right to the point. We're searching for a woman named Ruby Cramden or anyone who might know what happened to her.

Ruby is important to a family I've come to represent. This family was told that she was dead and we have been doing some investigation to find the body of Ruby Cramden."

She shrugged hopelessly. "What makes you think I'd know anything about this Ruby?"

By this time, Bosco was done playing games. "Please don't think me rude, but I think Ruby Cramden is alive and I am pretty sure we have found her. Would you agree…Ruby …?"

She looked at him with the eyes of an animal caught in a trap. "So, what if I am Ruby Cramden. I don't know anyone who would want to find me. If you're any kind of investigator, you must know I was in prison and am just a worthless ex-convict…no family to speak of…my friend Emma died and now my friend Luis is dead too. Why would anyone be looking for me?" Tears rimmed her eyes, the eyes so identical to Abigail's, but she quickly wiped the tears away.

"Ruby…if I may call you Ruby?" In an indication she had no defense left, the woman waved her hand helplessly. Bosco continued, "I've been in police work all my life and I know for a fact that just because someone has been in prison, they are not necessarily worthless. Often after prisoners have served their sentences, they leave prison deciding they are going to make something of their lives. Why do you feel like you're worthless and that no one would want to know about you?"

Her immediate response was a look that briefly defined her red-haired personality, but just as quickly her face softened. "Do you realize I spent the early years of my life on the streets, eating food from garbage cans behind restaurants and doing things for money I don't even want to think about? What kind of a chance do I have to make something of my life…especially now that Luis is dead?"

Pastor Petrov had been sitting quietly watching her compassionately and he knew he couldn't keep out of the conversation any longer.

"Ruby, think of what you're good at. What do you enjoy doing? What could you do to earn a living that would make you happy and proud?"

Following his question there was such a long pause that the pastor wondered if she had heard him or just wasn't interested in answering.

Slowly, she became more animated and responded, "I found out I like gardens. I like to plant things and see them grow…it's almost like having children as I nourish each flower or vegetable." She stopped short, realizing she had opened up to people she didn't know, but the pastor had such a godly presence that somehow she thought it would be all right to tell some of her secret hopes.

"Yes, that's what I could do. I think I'm good at it, and I really like gardening."

"Now, see? You're not worthless at all, are you?"

A half smile crossed her face, but just as quickly she sobered again. "So, what about this family that's trying to find out about me? I've been here a long time, and Luis…Dr. Minolo…told me I've had amnesia. Did you know that from your investigation, detective?"

"Actually, we just learned today that you are Ruby Cramden and that you're alive. Our whole investigation so far has been to find the *body* of Ruby Cramden."

"Why did you think I was dead?"

"For some reason Dr. Minolo told me that when I talked to him."

"Why would he do that? He knew I was here all the time and that I couldn't remember anything."

"Ruby," Bosco answered as carefully as possible, "I think Dr. Minolo…Luis…told me that so I wouldn't look for you. I think he wanted to protect you, and I also think just maybe he wanted to keep your friendship and didn't want anything to disturb that."

"He was especially good to me all these years and we were dear friends."

Pastor Petrov interjected, "It sounds like you've remembered more things now. Do you think your memory is coming back?"

"Yes, it is, but some of the things I wish I didn't remember. You men are complicating my life. I really don't want anyone to know about me. How can I let myself get involved with something from my past? I want to forget most of it."

"Ruby," the pastor responded, "would you tell us about yourself, about your past. We're interested and concerned about you."

Even though her attitude was somewhat defiant, she was feeling more at ease by the pastor's compassion and sincerity. She had to admit that as restrained as she had planned to be, she was truly impressed by his manner. *I think he really does want to help.*

They discussed her amnesia, the care Dr. Minolo had given her, and how he had arranged for her to be a companion for his aging mother in the friendly little cottage. Ruby was reluctant to discuss her prison past, but after much reassuring she explained the reason for her imprisonment that caused her feelings of unworthiness.

"When those memories returned of my prison life, I felt awful. I sure don't feel worthy to see or talk to anyone. I'm a loner anyway and after my dear friend, Emma, died I had no desire to make friends here in the village. I'm content the way things are and I don't want the problems that my background might cause."

Pastor Petrov straightened up and it was obvious he was going to start a new subject of discussion. "Ruby, have you ever had a faith in Jesus Christ?"

She tried to get her memories organized before answering. "There's a woman I remember. Her name was Dorie, and she was my friend. I don't know where she is now, or if she's even alive, but I remember she talked about Jesus and how she was beginning to believe in him. After we talked about it, I started thinking I wanted to believe too. I never had any religious training or anything, so I guess that doesn't mean much."

The pastor smiled at Ruby. "I'd like to tell you of God's great love for you and each person through his Son, Jesus Christ." Ruby listened intently as the pastor continued to relate how each human ever born is sinful. Ruby nodded in agreement, knowing how she had sinned through her life.

"But, God is a Holy God and he cannot tolerate sin. He wanted to enjoy those he created, so he planned that Jesus would go to the Cross and die in the place of all people. In other words, Jesus suffered, died and rose again from the dead so that he could pay the penalty for all *our* sins."

"I remember something about that," Ruby interjected, "but if Jesus did that, then what are we supposed to do to pay him back?"

Detective Boscovich got up from the table where he had been sitting and joined the conversation. "That's the great part, Ruby. We don't have to do anything to pay Jesus back for saving us and making us worthy to be God's children. All he wants us to do is to believe in him and live our lives as his friends."

Ruby listened and quietly thought about what she had heard. It fit with what she was beginning to remember about talks she and her friend had years ago. She knew she wanted a faith in God, but she had a lot to think about before deciding to accept God's forgiveness for the awful things she had done. How could she feel free of all that?

It would take a while for Ruby Cramden to understand that because she believed in Jesus, she *already* was worthy of that love.

The afternoon visit ended as Bosco went to his car to get a Bible for Ruby to use until she was able to get one.

Pastor Petrov took Ruby's hand in his and spoke softly. "Ruby, I know Dorie was your friend. She thought you had died in that shooting and was very concerned your body be taken care of properly. She asked me to check into it for her because she had to leave the country to see if she could help her husband."

Ruby smiled as she thought about her friend, and the pastor continued, "I'm sorry to have to tell you, Ruby, but we just learned that she and her husband were both killed in a car accident a year ago. I'm truly sorry. She was a friend of mine too."

Ruby wiped away the tears that were beginning to flow. She had finally remembered her friend after all these years, and now she was gone. "Goodbye, my friend," she whispered.

Bosco returned with the Bible and as Pastor Petrov stood to leave, he casually asked if they might come again to visit sometime soon.

Ruby was on the spot. How could she say no? She wasn't sure if she wanted to talk more. The memories that had returned and her friend Luis' death was all she could handle at the moment. But, looking into the sincere eyes of the pastor, she had to say something, so she nodded and said "Maybe."

As the two men left, Bosco turned and took her hand, kissing it in a gesture of respect for a worthy lady.

Driving out of the yard they could barely make it to the road into the village before letting out shouts of thanks.

Chapter Thirty-nine

The call came as Abby and David were finishing a quiet dinner in Abby's suite. Bosco was on the line. He wanted to share his good news but had decided not to divulge any information over the phone about what he and the pastor had discovered. He planned to be noncommittal until just the right time. So, he called Abby with an invitation.

"I hope you're not feeling discouraged, Abby. I can tell you my investigation is going well, in fact I want you to know that I'm not sure if Dr. Minolo was telling you the truth when he told you about Ruby and how she died. Perhaps we can talk about it tomorrow if you and your young man would be free to meet?"

"Oh yes, I'm sure David and I could make it tomorrow," she glanced quickly at David for his approval. "But Bosco, if Dr. Minolo lied what would that mean?"

"I'm not sure yet, Abby, but we can talk about it more tomorrow. Pastor Petrov has a call to make in the Village of Semsk tomorrow at 2:00 and as the weather should be pleasant, I thought we could give the pastor a ride and do our visiting at the same time. We could pick you up at 1:00?"

"That's just fine. One it is then."

She and David sat cozily on the window seat overlooking the park and she filled him in on her conversation with Bosco and the plans for a meeting.

"So much has happened in such a short time," Abby sighed as she mentally retraced her journey.

"As I think about it, David, I have learned a lot about my background. I've met Ruby's father and discovered things about Ruby's past. And, you know, I like the old man. He was sorry for his past mistakes and maybe he'll even try to change.

I'm planning to see him again soon and tell him who I really am." She smiled at the recollection of the scruffy, frail man.

"Through my talk with Donna Ranno, the nurse I told you about, and Dr. Minolo, I have a much better understanding of how I was formed. It's still almost impossible for me to imagine that I am the person that Dr. Krebsny formed in a lab, but as time goes on I just pray I'll be able to accept it.

"Those are positive things that I can think about in the future. And, I am so thankful that I'm able to accept what our friend, Pastor Petrov, told me…that no matter what circumstances surrounded my birthing, I am still loved by God and still saved through his Son, Jesus."

David squeezed her hand. "You and I will take care of any loose ends there may be in your search, and we'll do it together. You'll never have to face any of this alone again."

Looking into David's eyes she added, "David, the fact that you love me just as I am is the happiest part of my search."

As she leaned on his shoulder her face saddened for a moment. "I just wish I knew for certain what happened to Ruby…if I just knew …" and her voice trailed off in whispered tones.

When Bosco and the pastor picked up the young couple, Bosco mentioned the news of Dr. Minolo's death to Abby in case she hadn't heard. Yes, she had heard and felt surprisingly sad at the news.

"I don't mean to minimize his death and I don't mean to be crass, but do you think this will affect our finding Ruby's body?"

Bosco smiled to himself, assuring her it should make no difference whatsoever.

After a quiet reflection, the remainder of the ride to Semsk was enjoyable. The beauty of the area was slowly erasing thoughts about the investigation until Abby remembered her phone conversation with Bosco and asked when they would be reviewing all the information he had gotten.

Bosco had a difficult time replying without actually giving her an answer, but before he had to worry about it, Pastor Petrov quickly began telling the story of Abby as a two-year-old and how she had captivated the women of the choir when Abby and her mother sought shelter there.

It was enough for Abby to forget for a minute that her question hadn't been answered and she listened attentively. David, on the other hand, was wondering why Bosco seemed to be evading her question. He finally decided there must be a good reason, and he would ask about it if there was an opportunity to speak privately.

As they arrived in Semsk, Bosco drove straight through the village into the country as if he knew just where he was going. Abby wondered about that and was just about to ask when Pastor Petrov spoke up. "There's the cottage. Drive right into the driveway, Bosco."

"Is this the person you had your appointment with, Pastor?" Abby asked. As the pastor nodded Abby pointed out the quaint cottage. "You know, this cottage is a lot like my little 'Hansel and Gretel' house in Vesta."

Pastor Petrov got out of the car and turned to Abby as if he had just had a good idea. "Would you mind coming with me, Abby? I'm counseling the woman who lives here, and although I'll only be a minute she might feel more at ease with another woman present."

Abby, happy to be of help, got out of her side of the car and began walking to the door of the cottage with the pastor. What she didn't realize was that as they walked, the pastor lagged a bit behind her so when she reached the door, Abby was standing on the step alone, with the pastor a short distance behind.

She knocked timidly, waiting for the door to open.

Chapter Forty

Arthur Cramden faced doors in his life that he wasn't sure he wanted to open. He hadn't been the same since that young woman had found him. The memory of her intertwined with faded memories of his daughter, Ruby, and that worried him. *She looks so much like Ruby did the last time I saw her.* Abigail's face appeared in his mind more and more often until he offhandedly decided maybe she was Ruby's kid. *But, why wouldn't she say so if Ruby was her ma?* At times, it was just too much for the old man.

The other door he was facing since that visit was the one he would someday have to open either to heaven or to hell, as Abigail had told him. He had read some of that book she left him. Some times when he read it, he felt good…like maybe he could believe in this Jesus and what the book said he had done for everyone who believed in him. But, there were other times after reading he was fearful and wondered about this place of the damned.

The day after Abigail had left, he was reading the book in the lobby of the shelter and some of the guys sitting near him began making fun of him, asking him if he was going to be a "Jesus freak," so after that he made sure he was always alone when he read. The problem with reading that book was he didn't always understand it which frustrated him even more, so he decided he'd find somebody who could help explain it to him.

After breakfast one morning, he left the shelter and walked down the street toward his bridge when he spotted a church. That church had been there for years, but today was the first day that Arthur Cramden ever really noticed it.

Somebody there should be able to answer some questions for him, so he started up the cement steps to the double wooden door. Suddenly, he lost his nerve and turned to leave. At that very moment the door creaked open and a man with a yellow broom in his hand stepped out. He was dressed in a flannel shirt and jeans, and he had such an enthusiastic greeting that Arthur was caught off guard.

"Hi there. Glad to see you," the man said approaching Arthur. "Just came out to sweep the front steps, but I'm glad to see someone to talk to so I have an excuse not to work." He stretched out his hand to Arthur who looked at him hesitantly before returning the handshake.

"From around here?" the man questioned in a friendly manner.

"Well…I…I stay at the shelter up the street sometimes," Arthur responded as he shifted from one foot to the other.

"Glad to meet you. I'm Tom, the pastor of this church. What'd you say your name was?"

"Arthur," he stammered. "My name is Arthur."

"Well, Arthur, I could sure use a good cup of coffee. Want to join me over at the café down the street? I'd like some company. Being a pastor can get pretty lonely sometimes. What'd you say?"

Arthur didn't know what to say and as he turned his head away from the young man, the pastor clapped him on the shoulder and steered him down the steps toward the café.

That morning, Arthur decided, was the best morning of his life. He had made a real friend in Pastor Tom, and over three cups of steaming coffee, Tom helped him to come to know the very best friend Arthur would ever have.

So that's what that Abigail was talkin' 'bout...how I should grab on to that preserver thing so I could be saved from drownin'. When I told Tom that story, he explained just like she did that if I believe in Jesus, I'll be saved from hell and go to heaven when I die. Boy, that Jesus is really somethin'!

Chapter Forty-one

Abby knocked again, this time a little more firmly, not realizing the pastor had stepped back to join Bosco and David and the three of them were watching with the excitement of teen-age boys at a football game.

Still no one came to the door, so after knocking one more time, Abby slowly began to turn away. Suddenly the door opened.

There was a brief moment of silence…then the moment of recognition. One word pierced the quiet afternoon, settling briefly on the cozy cottage and then drifting out over the meadows.

"RUBY!"

There before Abby stood a woman, the very likeness of the person Abby looked at in the mirror every day. Her red hair touched with gray cascaded to her shoulders, and her eyes revealed the same, but somewhat aging, beauty of Abby's deep blue eyes. Abby stood there immobilized. Ruby! It was Ruby! After her long, disparaging search, here was her Ruby!

Ruby stood in the doorway and heard the joyful sound of her name echoing over the countryside. As she looked into the eyes of the young woman standing before her, it was as if she was looking into a mirror of years past. This young woman was the image of herself. Her mind could barely comprehend what she was seeing.

It's ME…she's just like me…like I used to be…

Within seconds she knew. This was the beautiful child of her memories…the child she had longed to see. Instantly, the confining shell which had long surrounded Ruby broke away and all those lonely years were finally over.

"Abigail!" she cried. "My dear, sweet Abigail."

Abby's heart was overflowing as she reached for Ruby and they embraced in a love long overdue.

Epilogue

A year later, Abigail Demitt blissfully walked down the aisle of the Community Christian Church in Vesta on the arm of her older brother Stephen. She looked dazzling in the white flowing gown her mother, Dorie, had worn years before. She carried a single red rose for love found.

In the front row seat of honor sat Ruby, glowing with happiness for her dear Abby. After years of loneliness, she finally had a special, loving place in Abby's life.

Although there was a deep sense of loss without Dorie and Peter at the wedding celebration, the family knew this is what they would have wanted.

Next to Ruby sat Sarah, who though her age was taking a toll, was joyfully sharing Abby's wedding day.

As the organ played and Abby glided down the aisle to the cadence of the Wedding March, a rather unconventional wedding guest slipped unnoticed into a back row. He was an old man, dressed in a suit slightly large for his thin frame, but he had a broad smile that even his scruffy, gray beard couldn't hide.

As Abigail approached the altar, she could see her brother Josh facing her with a proud look of brotherly love, holding his Bible as he waited for her.

Next to Josh was her love, David. She could hardly contain her excitement as she gazed at him. He looked more handsome than she had ever seen him, and the intimate smile he gave her as she neared reaffirmed her identity as his true love.

She took David's hand and they walked toward Josh. Abby glanced at the Cross and knew she had found her identity as the Lord's love as well.

The past year had been an answer to many prayers. It brought about a gradual reconciliation between Ruby and Arthur Cramden. Though she continued to live in her farm home in Semsk, she frequently visited with those she loved in the States. She and Pastor Petrov had a most promising friendship, but no friendship was equal to the one she had found with her Savior.

Cindy and Josh were planning their upcoming wedding, and Stephen and his boys were regulars at Josh's church while they decided on a church in their neighborhood of New York.

Sarah was the cherished matriarch of the family and loved every minute of it. Her apartment at the Vesta Senior Nursing Facility was busy with visitors and she basked in the love of her family.

The shadow's grip that had held Abigail so tightly was finally broken and she was encouraged to see new vistas of hope ahead.

Dorie and Peter would have been so pleased.

****

"Therefore if any man *be* in Christ, *he is* a new creature; old things are passed away; behold, all things are become new." 2 Corinthians 5:17 KJV

BOOK GROUP DISCUSSION GUIDE

In today's world, human cloning seems more of a possibility every day. The reality of it brings about a variety of opinions and emotions. As a discussion group, what are some of the feelings the subject of human cloning generate…morally, socially and spiritually?

Abigail's reaction to the news was one scenario. Are there other reactions which might be viable upon hearing something so unbelievable?

As Abigail searches for answers, do the characters she meets share enough information to understandably give her peace about herself? Which character seems to be the greatest help to her, and how? Did you have empathy for the characters of her past even though they weren't necessarily always honorable people? Describe.

Ruby is one of the main underlying characters. What are your thoughts about her story and her importance to the plot? How much does she define the book?

What are the thoughts about David's reaction to the news he learns from Abigail? Do his feelings ring true to life, or are there several other reactions he might have expressed?

Which character did you find the most likeable? Intriguing? Believable?

Are the characters introduced in a timely manner? Do they relate enough to the heroine and the story? Is there enough reality to the plot to make it believable in terms of human cloning?

Does the plot flow in an interesting and intriguing manner?

Does the consistency of Abigail's faith come through? Is the message of hope in Christ presented clearly enough to Arthur?

If you've read *Running From the Shadows,* does *Breaking the Shadow's Grip* continue the story to your satisfaction? In what ways?

If you haven't read *Running From the Shadows,* would this sequel spur your interest in reading it?

Does *Breaking the Shadow's Grip* give any insights into messages of hope that can be applied to living everyday lives, and if so what are they?

How would you describe your thoughts about the book and its take-away message?